About the Author

Zoe Lambert is a Manchester-based writer. She has an MA in creative writing from UEA and a PhD from MMU. She lectures part time at various universities and works freelance as a workshop facilitator. She has also worked as an activist on asylum seeker issues.

First published in Great Britain in 2011 by Comma Press
www.commapress.co.uk

'These Words are No More Than a Story About a Woman on a Bus' and 'The Breakfast She Had' first appeared in *Ellipsis 2* (Comma, 2006). 'Crystal Night' was specially commissioned for *Litmus: Short Stories from Modern Science*, edited by Ra Page (Comma, 2011). 'My Sangar' was commissioned by The Whitworth Art Gallery as part of their 2010 exhibition, *The Land Between Us*, in response to Donovan Wylie's photograph 'Northern Ireland, South Armagh, Golf 40, West View,' 2007. An earlier version of 'When the Truck Came' was commissioned and published by Cheshire Libraries as part of World Book Day 2009.

Lines from '33 Bullets' by Ahmed Arif, translated from the Turkish by Murat Nemet-Nejat, from EDA: AN ANTHOLOGY OF CONTEMPORARY TURKISH POETRY, edited by the translator, published by Talisman House Publishers, 2004. Reprinted by permission.

ISBN   1905583281
ISBN-13   978 1905583287

LOTTERY FUNDED

The publisher gratefully acknowledges assistance from the Arts Council England North West, and the support of Literature Northwest.

Set in Bembo 11/13 by David Eckersall
Printed and bound in England by MPG Biddles Ltd.

THE
WAR TOUR

by
Zoe Lambert

For my parents

Contents

These Words are No More Than a Story About a Woman on a Bus

THE WOMAN HEADING towards you is old. You're not sure how old. You don't spend long guessing. Old will do. You watch warily as she makes for the seat next to you at the back of the bus. She's wearing a beige anorak. From a distance it looks respectable. Up close the coat is stained, the cuffs are grimy, and inside the collar is streaked and grey. She sits down and you shift slightly, placing your briefcase on your knee. You open it and flick through the letters and bills you picked up from the mailbox. But it's too early to contemplate bills, so you roll yourself a cigarette for the walk to the office and wonder where you left your antihistamines. The woman is watching you and your briefcase, so you close it carefully and glance outside. The bus is caught in traffic on Candle Road. It's shuddering and shunting round the bollards.

They threw letters from the trains, she says, as if you were mid-conversation.

Deportees would push their notes through high, thin windows.

What? You mumble. Sorry?

Letters, she says. She begins to cough. Her coughs are harsh and wracking. She wipes her mouth with a stained handkerchief. She grasps your hand, her fingers digging into your palm. You try to free your hand from the scaly feel of her skin. You notice her hands are scarred, the skin

1

stretched shiny and tight. Old scars. You worry about your personal space. She doesn't understand this; her knees press against your suit trousers, her breath is sharp and bitter on your cheek.

On her courier trips, she says, she'd find the notes, frozen and crisp by the train tracks. Sometimes wet with blurred ink scrawls. She'd leave them on the verges, like paper gravestones, with pebbles on the corners. Her father travelled on one of those trains. But she never found a note.

Where's this? you ask, loosening your tie.

Lithuania.

You think of Eurovision. Or is that Latvia? You draw a blank.

Her name, she says, is Elena Vidugirytė. She frowns at the ceiling as if she is picking a story from the air. Jonas Zemaitas, she says. Jonas Zemaitas.

She will tell you about Jonas.

You're not sure you want to know about Jonas. Or why she is telling you. Perhaps you should get off the bus to escape her, but your hangover plus hayfever won't let you stand. You rub your eyes and grunt.

This is all she needs.

Jonas, she says, was the commander of the Southern Partisan District. She met him when she joined the partisans with her brother, Jurgis. They volunteered after their father, the Mayor of Ukmerge, was deported, after they were moved from their villa to a tiny cottage on the edge of the town.

But it's the end she remembers, she says. The end.

The last time she saw Jonas she was delivering a message to his group in the forests near to Ukmerge. She was a messenger, a courier, between the groups of partisans in the area.

She remembers, she says, that the only noise was the rain on the leaves and the soft crunch of her boots on the forest floor. Around her the trees were tall and spindly, with a canopy of leaves, leaving the grass yellowing and patchy underneath. She remembers climbing over a fallen branch. She clutched her skirt. It was sodden and heavy and water trickled down her neck. She was so wet she wanted to cry.

She should have been used to creeping through the forest at night. But she wasn't. The darkness scared her; one of the strange, jagged shadows beyond the glow of her lamp could be a *velnias* with their riddles and their tricks. Or worse, Russians. They searched the woods for the partisans with their dogs and their lamps and informers' lies. They were picking off the partisans in ambushes. A week before, three in Jonas' division had been captured and taken to the prison in Vilnius.

Elena tucked in her scarf. She wanted to be by the fire with her mother, a glass of vodka and some fried bread. Her mother had begged her not to do this. Jorgis' decision she had not questioned, but Elena's she couldn't understand. It left her alone at night, sleepless and praying with a small illegal cross.

By day, Elena and her mother weaved for the collective. The former weavers, women who now had authority, examined and criticised their work. They'd throw their cloths on the floor of the cottage and wipe their boots on the weave of bourgeois wives. They'd grip and squeeze Elena's hands and denounce them as not the hands of workers.

Her mother would retell the old myths as they weaved, especially the tricks *laumes* would play on women like that. *Laumes* loved weaving, but when they were mistaken for bourgeois wives, they'd cast a spell on the spiteful women's thread, so it continually unravelled. Every cloth the women touched fell apart.

You find yourself half-listening, even though passengers are glancing over and raising their eyebrows at the woman's loud accent. You can feel the beginnings of a headache and the itch in your eyes is unbearable. You give in and rub.

3

Don't rub, she says.

On each trip she had to go a different route. That night she skirted round the mounds of unmarked graves. The soil was still fresh and she'd heard the dead had dug the pits themselves. Then she followed the stream northeast to where Jonas and his group were camped. The note almost hummed in her pocket, the words heavy and resonant against her hip. She was not supposed to read it. Not supposed to know. But she had. She always did. In case it said something about Jonas or Jurgis. And this one did.

She could hear barking in the distance. Barking meant Russians and their dogs. But it was far away. She stopped and listened. There were voices. What was that? '*Pasmikst, pakabakst?*'

She was shaking, but it was them of course. They weren't far. She followed the voices till she saw the lights of their cigarettes and the low-burning lamp.

Elena came out shyly, and stood on the edge of the clearing. '*Labas.*'

'*Labas.* Did you bring any *cepelinai*?' Jonas asked, approaching her.

'Just bread. Sorry. And some ham.'

Last time she had hugged him. This time he didn't wait. He was already under the tent with Feliksas and Pranuté. They were wet and bedraggled in their patched overcoats, with pustules and sores on their faces. They barely said hello. Elena saw that the second tent, where the others had been, was empty. The roof had collapsed on one side and was covered by yellowing leaves. Underneath a puddle had formed and four stones had been placed there, like graves.

'Come over, then. Get under here.'

She walked round the puddle in the middle of the clearing.

'You could fish in that,' she said and crouched next to Jonas. She handed him the message and the bread and ham. They bit into the small loaves, barely chewing large

4

mouthfuls. She watched Jonas read and eat at the same time. Then he focused on the bread. His face was streaked with dirt, yellow decay edged his teeth, and his knuckles were cracked and sore. His hands were shaking. His hands always fluttered and fidgeted, touching his forehead and his neck. The few times they had walked into the bushes together, she'd stroked his neck till he was calm.

Jonas read the note again, and tucked it into his coat pocket. She watched to see his reaction, but he just looked cold and tired. She edged nearer and took his hand.

'Are you alright?'

'Yes.' He freed his hand and scratched a weeping bite on his wrist.

Before, she thought, they would have been married by now. She tried to imagine him indoors, sitting at a table, the stove burning, and in another room, a neatly made bed. She tried to picture him standing by the fire in the old villa. She couldn't. In her mind, he drifted out of the window and floated into the woods, as if he were a *laumiukas*.

She knew that he grew up in a village south of Vilnius and that he'd graduated from the Kavnas Military School just before the war. In an old military photo he'd shown her, he had close-cut blonde hair, a smooth shaved chin and a wide open smile. She'd asked if she could keep the photo, but he said no. It was too risky.

They had met seven times. That was all. She'd sewn special epaulettes for his coat. He loved them. She'd brought him as much food as she could, sometimes taking from her mother's larder or saving him the meat from her plate. On her missions, she wasn't supposed to dawdle, but immediately return with the message. Jonas would walk with her for a little of the way. But after a few minutes he'd become fretful and want to get back to the others.

Elena wondered if he thought of her when she was not there, or if she disappeared from his mind, like a *laume* at the end of a tale.

5

The last time they met, they'd argued. Usually, she stayed quiet. That night, she couldn't. Jonas had said that the Lithuanian government had just given into the Russians. It had been weak. They'd tried to bargain, but were tricked and either sent to Siberia or shot. That was no loss; they'd done nothing for Lithuania. And everyone knows not to bargain with devils. Elena thought it was more complicated than that. Things always were. She'd said this and he'd sneered. That was the talk of conspirators, he said. Things were never so complicated as not having a choice. Capitulate or fight. They should have fought. There was always a choice. He was angry. She didn't know how someone could stay so angry all the time.

'Not always,' she said. She was thinking of her father, locking himself in the mayor's office till they came for him.

'Women,' he said. 'That's a woman talking.'

'Do you have a reply?' she asked as he fingered the note. Jonas nodded and scribbled, sealing it in an envelope.

'You should get back. You must be tired,' he said.

'Yes. I should.' She crouched, as if to stand. 'Goodbye then,' she said and then more loudly, as if pointing something out. 'Goodbye, Jonas.'

She walked across the clearing. He was leaving. He had to take the regiment further south, to group with other divisions near Vilnius. It was out of her area. Too far for her to walk. Leaving, like that. No goodbye, nothing. As if she were nothing. She was angry then. 'Jonas?' she said, even though the others looked up.

'What?'

'When will I see you?'

'I don't know.'

'You were going to go? Just like that? Without saying anything?'

'Why? Have you read the message?'

'No, I…'

He turned away. 'You should go,' he said.

She grabbed her lamp and ran into the woods. He didn't follow, even though she looked behind to see if he would. She walked, holding the lamp in front of her, its pool of light flickering. It was darker here, the foliage thicker. She wasn't sure where she was. Perhaps she should go back towards the clearing and retrace her steps home in the other direction, past the stream. Then she saw that she was at the stream. How did she get here? It was shallow with stones. She could cross. But the bank was muddy. She slipped on the verge, her lamp shattering and her hands deep in the mud. She lay there. The sound of the water trickling was soothing in the dark. Further along – she wasn't sure in which direction – the stream was wide and nearly still. On a bright day, the sun would shoot through the leaves and branches, the trees casting dark shadows on the water.

She didn't know whether to go back or follow the stream. She pulled herself out of the mud and wiped her hands on her skirt. She wanted to return to the clearing, but there was nothing to be said. Tomorrow, she'd continue weaving with her mother and again the day after that. She'd carry on delivering messages but Jonas would be gone. The message. She slid the note out of the envelope. She tried to read the words but they were blurred. His hands had been shaking and the scrawl said nothing. She folded it in the envelope and carefully put it in her pocket.

She heard barking, far off. She listened and eventually she heard guns. She heard voices, shouts and more shots. She should run, get away, hide. Perhaps they'd look for her as well. But her legs were weak. She huddled against a tree, her knees to her chest, shivering.

How had the Russians found them? The others could have talked. There had been rumours about the prison in Vilnius. Stories of a room where they made you stand naked on a small ledge above a floor of ice. But she didn't believe they would talk. She held onto the tree trunk, her cheek pressed against the smooth, wet bark. From somewhere she could smell smoke.

Later, she got up slowly, and feeling her way, she walked back to the clearing. The clearing was not hard to find. It was lit by a dimming fire where the tent used to be. Footprints and tracks scoured the mud. All the equipment, the bowls, the blankets had been dragged into the fire.

She didn't get home till morning. Her mother had not slept. She was waiting in the kitchen, pacing up and down. She bandaged Elena's hands and gave her a large vodka. You will have to go, she said. You will have to leave.

The bus shudders and stops. You grab the seat in front of you. She grasps your forearm, her fingers crinkling your sleeve. Passengers are staring out of the windows, muttering to each other and rubbing at the glass. The driver seems to have disappeared. You worry vaguely about being late for work. She uprights herself and examines her scarred hands, turning them in front of her.

She can see Jonas, she says, coughing. She can always see him, even now, crouched in the tent, biting into the hard loaf, his hands fidgety, unsure. And later when she dragged him from the fire and laid him on the ground in the clearing. The epaulettes she'd sewn were black and burnt.

You try not to stare at her hands. You shift in your seat. Clear your throat. Glance down the bus. Some of the passengers are queuing to get off. Through the window, you watch them trailing, one after the other, past the school railings, to the bus stop at the end of the road.

You turn to her, clasping your briefcase, ready to leave. You're not sure what to do with this story, or what to say to Elena, the old woman sitting beside you on the bus.

From Kandahar

BY THE TIME Phil jumped off the bus at the top of Langworthy Road, he had a line of sweat along his back and patches under his arms. The air was muggy and close and wrong. Salford should not be this hot. He slung his oversized bag over his shoulder and walked down the road past his old primary school, listening to the screams and shouts from behind the red brick walls. Two teenage girls were staring at him from a corner; he wished he'd been able to change out of his uniform.

On the flight from Kandahar, all the lads had gone on about what they wanted to eat first. Phil wanted a Sunday roast, but it was a Monday and his mum had promised a surprise.

He turned left and then right onto Osborne Street. They were still trying to do the thing with the flowers to liven up the area: baskets hanging outside doors and pots on windowsills. A banner round his door said, 'Welcome Home Philip' in blue and red and little Union Jack flags poked out of the pots of gardenias. The door of his house was open but they didn't see him at first. The living room was full of his aunts and cousins. His mum was in the kitchen, peering in the oven, and his sister Wendy was rolling a cigarette by the back door. There were balloons and party poppers and paper bowls of crisps and cola bottle sweets, as if it was a children's party. Phil knocked on the open door and they all gushed at once.

'It's Phil! It's Phil!'

His mum hurried towards him, saying, 'Look at you!' Aunt Jill took his bag, exclaiming how heavy it was, and her three boys tried to grab his camouflage trousers. One jumped on his toes, shouting, 'Can you feel it?' Room was made for him on the sofa next to Gran and a plate piled with sandwiches and chicken legs was put in front of him. Then they wanted to know all about it. What were the rations like? (Not bad). Where did he sleep? (In a sleeping pod). How hot was it? (Very hot). Did he have mosquito bites? (Loads).

'Let him eat his tea,' his mum said.

'Here, have a chicken leg,' Gran said, pushing her leftovers onto his plate.

'I'm OK...'

'Did your mum tell you I have a new doctor?' she said, spit working at the corners of her mouth. 'He's very good.'

'Hasn't Phil grown?' Aunt Jill shouted across the room, and Aunt Mel leaned over to knead his thigh. 'He certainly has.' She patted his cheek. 'Quite the young man now, isn't he, Jill? I told you didn't I? The army would be the making of him.'

Phil tried one of the sandwiches on his plate. Cheese and damp lettuce. He was going off this homecoming. That's what the lads said. As soon as you're home you want to get straight back out again.

'Might take these boots off,' he said to the room.

'You've not finished your food.'

'I'll be back in a minute.' They all watched him go for the stairs. He could hear them on the landing. 'He looks like he's grown, doesn't he?'

In his room, Phil pulled off his uniform and boots and found his favourite t-shirt and jeans in the drawer. Perhaps if he stayed up here, they'd all go home. *I can't believe the change in your bedroom*, his mum had said when he returned from training. He'd lined up the new trainers he'd bought with his first wage in their boxes and hung all his t-shirts and shirts in the same direction. She'd caught him ironing his jeans and got all excited. But the mess in the kitchen had bugged him. No one ever washed up.

'Philip?' his mum called. 'Are you coming down? The chilli's ready.'

The army will be the making of you (his aunt said). *Make him learn some discipline. You'll learn some skills* (his mum). *You don't even need any GCSEs to get in. They'll take anyone* (Wendy).

Cheers Wendy. He had his GCSEs. He'd left school and not been able to find a job. He wanted to earn some money, but each job was worse than the last. Salford Market (boring, just standing there). The chicken factory (fucking awful). McDonald's (worse). So he'd dossed at home, and then his mum had dropped army leaflets on his knee (thanks, Mum!) But then he'd gone on the website and it had surprised him. Good pay. Get to see the world. Training in Canada and Corfu. *Think Soldier.* He'd tried out the interactive stuff. *What would you do?* When he left for Catterick, he couldn't wait to get started.

But he wasn't daft. He got what they were doing with the training, not trying to break you, but push you till you fought back as a team. Kind of like fighting against them, but doing what they wanted. He'd realised this a few weeks in. He'd been out on exercise with 20 kilos on his back. He was dragging behind the others in his team and stopped to catch his breath and lean against a tree. He had a stitch that was eating into him. He could see them all running up the hill with their compasses and maps, shouting encouragement to each other. All he wanted was to curl into a ball and fuck them off. He crouched down and began to wriggle out of his backpack. But then Jonno ran back down the hill, shouting, 'Come on Phil!' He grabbed Phil by the arm and roared in his face, and they both went, 'Raaaaaaaa!' and ran up the hill, screaming like girls.

Phil laced up his blue and white Adidas trainers, and jumped down the stairs. His mother was at the bottom, holding out a bowl of chilli.

'Here you are,' she said. 'Just how you like it.'

'I'm going out for a bit,' he said, squeezing past her.

His aunts and cousins looked up from their plates. 'Oh, he's taken his uniform off,' one said.

'Phil, please,' his mum said. 'Why can't you...'

Phil held his hands up, as if he was being attacked. 'I'm just going out. OK?'

At the end of Osborne Street, Phil walked towards the grassy play area where the houses were bombed in the war. He could hear the building work on the next street. Further down, whole streets of terraces had metal-plated windows and doors. He turned back onto Langworthy and walked up to the Height. John would be at the Hound and Pheasant at five. John and Phil went way back. John worked at the Argos on the Precinct, and he was already assistant manager. He'd been all, 'Soz, but you won't hack it, mate.' So Phil said, 'Why don't *you* join?' and he said, 'I don't need to prove anything.'

Phil didn't have anything to prove either. But all through the training it had felt as if he had. He and the 1 Lancs had checked in like you did on a normal plane and flown from Brize Norton to the airport in Kandahar. He had seven hours of Hicks telling him about Genghis Khan, the Soviets and everybody else who'd invaded Afghanistan, and Jonno going on about how he couldn't wait for some action, and showing off pictures of his girlfriend. In Kandahar, they flew in a Hercules to Camp Bastion. Phil liked it there; it was like a Trafford Centre in the desert. A few days later they were driven to their forward operating base in Sangin. Inside the Mastiff, they stared at the floor, under the thin, green light. Phil was on edge, feeling like a sitting duck, and thinking of all the roadside bombs and IEDs that were waiting to be rolled over. Hicks went on about the blast attenuating seats, while Phil swayed back and forth, the lads' heads looming in his face. He undid his helmet and was sick in it. The others moaned, 'Fucking hell, Phil.' He could hear a couple of them retching. His head swam and he had to hold his helmet of sick all the way to the patrol base, trying not to spill it. He was 'Puking Phil' after that. *Puker. You puked yet, Phil?*

He walked past the shops on Bolton Road; the off licence, the tattooist where Wendy had one done on her shoulder, the Greggs. He'd had to work hard after the puking incident. But he didn't show himself up again. The forward operating base wasn't like Camp Bastion at all. They were on 24 hour ration packs and slept in doss bags under mosquito nets, but Jonno said this was why they were here: to be in the thick of it, not all cosy with their own Pizza Hut.

Phil put his head in the pub door. After the shootings last year, they were trying to smarten up the Hound and Pheasant, but it wasn't working. It was the same old shit hole, stinking of piss and stale beer. They needed to get rid of the multicoloured disco lights for starters. The ripped pool table and games machine were still there. The music was blaring inside and the lights flickered around a small empty dance floor. John was in a corner chair with a pint. Phil went over, saying, 'John. How you doing? What's with the work shirt?'

'It's the look of a manager.' John sat with his elbows resting on the back of the chair, his nipples straining through the material. 'And where's your kit?'

'I'm not walking round looking like a squaddie. Not round here.'

'You've wimped out more like.' John laughed and took a swig.

Phil took a breath. 'You alright for a drink?'

'Yeah. Got this, mate.'

Phil bought a pint and went out back for a smoke. It was only six o'clock and four more mates were coming. There'd be a whole night of drinking and piss-taking, but he wasn't going back home to have his cheeks pinched.

The beer garden was like someone's backyard with the cheap metal tables and B&Q awning. He sat down with his pint, rolled up and watched the reddish, purple sky above the railings.

Out there, his least favourite job had been manning the sangar; you were constantly on edge, thinking every blur and movement in your night vision goggles was an insurgent. It was positioned on the edge of a village, which had been taken a few weeks previously. The bazaar was going again, and the embedded reporter had already blogged on the BBC with pictures of the locals holding sacks of almonds and dried apricots, with the first lieutenant putting his thumbs up. On patrol, Phil had heard the Special Forces coming in by Apache helicopter. It blew off the roof of a house as it landed in a field, and then left an hour later. Probably a search and detain op.

On the third or fourth night, Phil and Hicks were pacing up and down, and scanning the area around them with their night vision goggles. The green and black shapes morphed and blurred in front of Phil's eyes, while Hicks gave him a history lesson on the word 'sangar', about how it came from when the British were here in the nineteenth century. Then Hicks said, 'What's that?'

A man was climbing over an irrigation ditch. He stumbled across the field, tripping as if he was drunk on the ridges of the hardened dirt. Phil pulled off his goggles and flashed the spotlight on him. The man fell to his knees in the middle of the field.

'Stop!' Hicks called. 'What's the word for stop?' he whispered.

'I dunno. He has stopped.'

They flashed the light over him again. His face and body were soaked in blood.

'Lift your shirt.'

The man didn't move.

'We need an interpreter.'

'Radio for one.'

A few minutes later, the interpreter, called Abdul or Ahmed or something, arrived yawning and rubbing his eyes, along with some back-up. The man had sunk forward onto the ground. Hicks asked the interpreter to tell the man to show his chest. The interpreter spoke to the man, and the man sat up and drew up his tunic to show his narrow hips, protruding ribs and thick chest hair. Then the back-up put a black bag over the man's head, even though it was dark.

A lad came out the back of the pub. He was wearing baggy jeans, a bulky jacket and a woollen hat pulled low over his greasy hair. He was the spitting image of Phil when he was sixteen. The kid lit up and sipped his beer like he was the queen with a teacup.

The barman came out, adding pint glasses to his stack. Behind him was someone familiar. It was Barry from school. Phil didn't know how he wasn't in prison. At fourteen he'd forced skinny kids to burgle houses for him before he got into the exotic pet business.

'Oy, Phil. You back?'

'Hi Barry.'

His head was shaved and on his fat neck he'd had a tattoo done of a shark and a diver. Barry stepped nearer, peering at Phil. 'So did you find Osama?'

Phil ground out his cigarette in the ashtray, while Barry leaned against the wall behind him. 'You back the big hero?'

'You what?'

'Cause I heard you just went round killing kids.'

'You need to get your facts right, civvie.'

'Who are you calling a fucking civvie?' Barry walked behind Phil's chair and clipped the back of his head. 'Fucking cadet!'

'Piss off.' Phil pushed his chair back and sprang up.

Barry stood his ground. 'Kiddie killer.'

And then it was all over; the barman must have heard the clatter of the chair and came out, pointing at Barry. 'You! Enough!'

Barry held up his hands, like he was innocent, then pulled up his collar over his tattoo and sauntered inside.

'He's alright until he's had a few,' the barman said, going back in the pub.

Phil shrugged, trying to look like he wasn't bothered. But he couldn't sit down again. He needed to get out of there, avoid his mates, that dickhead, and go somewhere quiet. The woolly hat kid was still sitting there, watching and sipping his drink. Phil finished his pint, then he moved a chair next to the wall, stepped on it and jumped over the wall into the car park. There were no cars, just a pile of tires. The kid landed behind him, stumbling.

'What do you want?'

'Where you off to?'

'Nowhere.'

He walked to the road and peered round the corner. The kid was behind him. 'Are you a squaddie?' he asked.

'No.'

'Yeah, you are.'

Phil could see Barry on Bolton Road with two other lads, so he walked up King's Road. The lad followed him, saying, 'Tell us then, tell us what it was like.'

'It wasn't like anything.'

Phil turned around. He could see they were following him, so he strode past the church and library. At the end of the road, he turned left and then right onto Godfrey's. The kid was still tagging behind him, so he said, 'I used to have that jacket.'

'Did you?'

Phil could tell he was impressed. 'Yeah. But I wouldn't be caught dead in it now.' He carried on walking. He'd go to Light Oaks Park and see if there were any ducks left.

'Are we going to the park?' the kid asked. 'Want a can?' He pulled out a Heineken from his jacket and another for himself. 'Go on,' he said. 'It's not poisoned.'

Phil took it and walked off down the road. An old witch was peering from behind her posh curtains – so he gave her the finger and carried on.

The kid caught up with him. Phil went through the park gates. He used to come here after dark when the gates were closed, and they'd climb through a hole in the railings. He strode down the path, past the basketball courts and towards the pond.

'So you gonna tell me or what?'

'There's nothing to tell.'

He squeezed through the bushes and crouched on the bank. The twigs crunched under his trainers; the ground wasn't too muddy, so at least it wouldn't ruin them. There was a family of ducks swimming across the pond, weaving around floating weeds and litter. He sipped his beer, trying to ignore the kid's chatter.

It had gone round the FOB that Phil and Hicks had successfully detained an insurgent. The lads clapped them on the back and they were given extra 24 hour ration packs. 'Like I'd want to eat any more of this,' Hicks said.

Phil was called to the Sergeant's tent a couple of days later. Sergeant John Parker was in his forties and reminded Phil of his old physics teacher. The sergeant told him that the insurgent that Phil had detained had given them useful information on the whereabouts of a cell. Special Forces were coming in and 1 Lancs were to provide support.

Phil's foot went into something soft. 'Fuck.' It was a duck lying on the ground with its head to the side and wing out, like it was one of those ducks you get on walls. Its chest was cut open and tiny bones stuck out. 'Fuck,' he said again. Blood and dirt were all over his trainer.

'Someone's killed it,' the kid said, kneeling down.

'Don't touch it!'

'We should bury it.'

'You're not fucking burying it.' Phil pulled back the branches; he'd heard voices.

Barry from the pub and another lad Phil didn't recognise were strolling up the path, looking from left to right.

'Let's go to the playground,' Phil said.

'Shouldn't we hide here?'

'I'm not hiding from them.' Phil watched Barry and the other one walk down the hill towards the gate, then he tried to wipe his trainer on the leaves. The kid was still standing next to the duck, kicking leaves over it.

'Come on,' Phil said. He kept wiping his foot on the grass, but the blood and dirt were ingrained on the white leather.

In the playground, all the swings were in action. There was a climbing frame and spongy tarmac, and a big roundabout with bars you could balance on. There were two swings for babies and two normal ones. Phil used to swing standing up. He'd come down here at night and do the usual: drink White Lightening and look out for Karen. He'd liked her for years, but she never came out except when she went knocking on doors. She was doing her A Levels now. Maybe he'd go past her house. He wished he hadn't bumped into Barry. He had never been one for fights, and he couldn't be bothered with one now.

'Where do you live?' Phil asked.

'Down Duchy Road.'

'War zone.'

'So did you get a medal?

Phil put his can on the ground and jumped on the roundabout. Pushing himself with his right foot, he perched on the bar and span round. 'Yeah.'

'Cool. What for?'

'Nothing. They just give them out.' Phil dragged his foot on the ground. The kid was standing near the roundabout and tried to grab it as Phil swung past.

'I'm gonna join up.'

Phil was going to say, 'You wouldn't last a minute,' but that's what they'd said to him, and he'd joined, so he said, 'I'm going on the swing.' He didn't swing himself though, he just hung there, examining his trainers.

Phil, Hicks, Jonno and four others from 1 Lancs had been deployed to the edge of Tansin, where they waited for Special Forces to arrive. Lance Corporal Williams was leading them. Their op was to search the houses around the bazaar for insurgents and possible IED caches. They were positioned around the remnants of a deserted compound beside the bazaar. They could hear the Apache in the distance. Phil fiddled with the control buttons on his night vision goggles and clipped them to his helmet.

'This is what I've come for,' whispered Jonno. 'This is it!' He turned to Phil. 'Tell you what, I'm going to propose when I get back.'

'Quiet,' said Williams.

The American marines made their way to the square, and 1 Lancs followed. Phil, Hicks and Jonno were positioned at each entrance of the square, armed with SA80 rifles. Phil was behind a pile of sandbags. Behind the empty market stalls there were four or five doorways. The marines separated into groups of three at each door. They rammed the doors open and disappeared inside.

1 Lancs waited and listened to the gunfire and the shouting and the screaming.

'Do you want us to go in?' Phil said into his mouthpiece.

'Keep your position,' Williams said.

There was screaming and the patter of machine gun fire, and then both petered out. Phil waited, hardly moving for ten minutes. No sound. Nothing. 'Fuck it,' he muttered and started to run, bowed, through the stalls. He stopped at the last stall, then ran for the nearest door. He edged it open with his rifle and stepped inside.

On the floor, a man was lying on his back motionless and two old women without their veils were sprawled beside him. Phil ran to the door of the next room to find the four marines bending over in a circle. One turned and opened fire, but Phil was behind the door. 'Friendly, friendly,' he shouted. The shooting stopped. 'Private Philip Nicholson, A Company, 1 Lancs.'

He edged back towards the door. The marine was facing him with his rifle in position. Behind him, another was bent over a body, his hands covered in blood. He turned towards Phil and said, 'Get back to your position, Private.'

Phil nodded and backed away. Outside, he went behind the sandbags and slumped down. Williams was going on at him in his earpiece. 'What the fuck was that? You don't just swan in on the SF!'

Phil and 1 Lancs crouched behind their sandbags, while the marines bustled in and out, finally closed the doors to the compound, and left in their Apaches. Then 1 Lancs headed back to the Mastiff, leaving the compound in darkness. Phil sat in the back, as the lads moaned about the lack of action.

'What did you see?' Jonno whispered. 'Go on.'

'Nothing,' Phil said. But the room had been full of dead bodies. Loads of them. Men of course, and they could have been insurgents, but there were also women and young boys, and there was loads of food, as if it was some sort of family party. The marine had been wearing plastic gloves and had a knife. His hands had been half dug in the corpse's stomach, pulling out a bullet. And he had put the bullet into a plastic bag.

Phil swayed back and forth in the vehicle, but he didn't feel sick anymore. He knew he wasn't going to say anything, even if he got disciplined for leaving his position. He would keep quiet; that was what you did.

Phil put out his cigarette. The music of an ice cream van was tinkling somewhere and a group of young girls were walking through the playground gate. It would be dawn now in Helmand, and Hicks and the others would be out on their morning exercise, joking and trying to trip each other up as they ran round the yard. Williams would be stood in the middle, shouting orders, while still clearly half asleep.

The kid came over and stood in front of the swing, with his hands inside his trousers. Phil pushed himself so the kid had to step backwards. 'Anymore of those beers?' Phil asked.

'One left,' the kid said, pulling it out of his jacket. 'So what do you do to join?'

Turbofolk

THERE WERE FREAK storms during the first summer of the war; wind burst through the streets of Belgrade, sweeping up table cloths and chairs. People cowered inside empty cafés as the rain lashed down. In the mornings, there were queues outside convenience stores for bread and sugar, and trails of cars to gas stations.

But it passed me by. I was seventeen and I couldn't stand it in Novi Belgrade. We lived in one of Tito's '60s suburbs, full of white, Legoland apartment blocks on wide, dusty roads, shadowed by the Ušće Tower. I spent my nights in bars on the Sava and slept in the daytime.

Towards the end of the summer, my brother, Dalivor, came home wearing a beret, saying he had joined the Volunteer Guard. He was off to Erdut for training with all the guys from his soccer club.

I was lying on the couch, watching an old comedy, and my mother was just home from RTV, where she scheduled prime time shows. Dalivor placed the beret on his head and admired his profile in the living room mirror.

'I can't believe you're joining up with that load of hooligans,' I said.

'Well, he's made his decision.' Mother kicked off her stilettos and lay back on the couch.

'I was watching that,' I said, as Dalivor flicked through the channels.

'Have you seen what they're doing?' he said. 'Killing children.'

The report was about Serbian children being slaughtered in Borovo Selo. There were shots of small bodies in bags. Forty-one dead.

Dalivor stood up, saying, 'I can't bear to watch this.' Mum sighed, rubbing her feet. Her toes were calloused and bent over like claws. I turned back to my comedy. My father was a journalist and we watched so much news that it no longer meant anything; I'd stopped believing a word they said.

At that time I was still wearing high heels, tall elaborate sandals that cut off my circulation. By the time I left Serbia, I'd thrown them out and only wore pumps or running shoes. That was 1996 and I'd enrolled on a BCom program in Commerce at the University of Toronto. As soon as I arrived I shaved my hair off. My mother cried when I told her, saying I'd never catch a rich Canadian looking like that.

I didn't visit much, maybe three times in ten years. I watched the Nato bombing from TVs in Toronto bars; saw the Ušće Tower burning. When I did visit, I'd just spend a couple of days with my parents till I couldn't bear the comments any longer: *Why can't you do something nice with your hair? Your studs make you look like a whore. Look at you! When are you coming home?* I didn't see my old friends. Not Maja or anyone from school. They were part of another life.

But now, I knock on our old front door. Mother opens it, hugging me briefly, and saying nothing about my hair or studs. It's 2008 and my father has had a stroke. I offered to come home to help out, so Aida and I flew to Budapest, where she took her train to Sarajevo and I got mine to Belgrade.

'Senka,' mother says, ushering me into my father's study. 'Senka. You won't believe what they're doing.'

'Who?'

'Those journalists at B92.'

I place my backpack on the floor. The study is a mess.

Papers are everywhere, piled on the desk and floor. Drawers are upturned and cupboards emptied. Mother's long brown hair is pulled back in a clip, revealing an inch of grey roots. Her collar bone juts out and her neck looks sinewy and old.

'It's just awful.' Her hands are shaking as she opens the files on my father's desk. She sits on the floor with them, then picks up documents and places them on the wooden boards. I crouch down next to her.

'How could someone do this?' she says. 'When your father is so ill.'

'Why? What've they got him for?'

She clutches the papers to her. 'If you're going to speak like that you might as well go back...'

I sigh loudly, so she sniffs and dabs at her eyes. 'I'm sorry,' she says. 'I really need you to look through these papers.'

There are piles and piles of them. A whole career's worth of articles, reviews, commentaries for newspapers, magazines, for *Politika* and *Vecernje Novosti*.

'So you want me to sort through them?'

'Those journalists just want to destroy people. It's disgusting. If he finds out, it will kill him.' She keeps on flicking through them, speaking more to herself. 'He is an esteemed intellectual. And now he lies in that bed...'

'So what did they say?'

'It's over there, on the chair.'

I really want to lie down, drink some beer, check my email. But I sigh and pick up the print out of the article: 'Media Warmongers Should Face Prosecution at the ICTY.'

Journalists, commentators, and members of the media should be taken to court for incitement to hatred... Many were nothing more than Milosevic puppets. Far too much 'information' published by the media in the early nineties consisted of nationalistic discourse and attacks aimed at people of other ethnicities... In the post-war years, numerous journalists have continued to deny Serbian war crimes. In particular, they have denied the Srebrenica genocide...

And below there is a list of names including my father's.

'Well, what do you think?'

I shrug my shoulders. 'What do you expect? It's come up before.'

The nurse knocks on the study door, saying that my father has been washed.

'Are you coming through?' Mother asks me.

'In a minute.' I drop my bag in my bedroom. It has been turned into a guest room, and the flowery decor makes me shudder. I slump on the bed to check my email on my laptop. There's nothing from Aida, but Maja has sent a message saying, "You're back!!!! Let's go for a drink!"

Maja. I flick through the photos of her. She's just the same. Deep tan, bleached hair. She sent me a friend request a few weeks ago and out of curiosity I accepted.

'Senka,' my mother calls. 'Are you coming?'

I close my laptop and go through. Mother whispers that he can't speak, and guides me over to the bed, as if I might not be able to find it.

My father is propped up on the pillows. His shoulders are thin under his blue pyjamas and one side of his face seems to have sagged. Only his hair is the same; thick and grey on his forehead, like waves on a painting. His eyes are yellow and slip over us.

'Bogdan,' she says. 'Bogdan. Senka's here.'

I hold his hand while Mother chatters on about me being home, that the nurses will be back to turn him, that they say he is improving. I wonder whether he knows about the journalists. His eyes close and his breathing changes. Mother pulls up the sheet, pats it and strokes his forehead.

'I'm going to have a lie down,' I say. 'I'm tired from the journey.'

Back in my room, I fling myself on the bed. During that summer I'd come in late, tiptoeing in the door at four or five with my sandals in my hand. The light would still be on in my father's study, and I could hear the murmur of the radio, which he'd switch off as I went past, though he never came out.

Most of the time he was quiet; he'd defer to my mother's chatter and rub her corns. It was always her with the opinions. My father saved his for his writing. He said nothing when she found Dalivor's balaclava stuffed in a coat pocket. She turned it over in her hands and put it back. And then Dalivor was gone. A few months later, successes in Vukovar were reported on the news and the Volunteer Guard were heroes, celebrities even. Father got drunk then, and ranted about a Greater Serbia, sitting at a stool in the kitchen while my mother chopped vegetables. He cried, 'Velika Srbija!' and had a toast on his own. I only caught snatches of it as I skulked past to the fridge. I was drawing inwards and planning my escape; one day I would study at a foreign university and get away from the war and everything.

I flick through photos on my phone of Aida. Her short, jagged hair, her heart shaped face. She hasn't contacted me at all. She'd cried when we were about to board our different trains from Budapest. Then we laughed and promised we'd meet back there in five days.

We met three years ago. I'd already dated a couple of women and one guy in Toronto, but none had lasted more than a few weeks. It was at The Eglinton Grand, an art deco movie theatre that had been turned into a banquet hall and convention centre on Eglinton Avenue. Both of us worked as waiters at a wedding, plodding back and forth from the kitchen with plates of salmon and artichokes. I'd catch her staring up at the curtain draped over where the old screen had been, and running her finger over the alabaster statues. We finished the bottles of champagne in the corridor behind the banquet hall till we were drunk and giggling, and stuffing leftover tiramisu into our mouths. 'So you're from Yugoslavia?'

'Yes,' she said. But we didn't need to ask which part. I asked her to come back to mine. I had some šljivovica and two shot glasses; she said she missed it more than anything, so we got the TTC to Kensington Avenue, where I shared an apartment with other students above the Coral Sea Fish Market.

We lay on the living room floor, knocking back the šljivovica, with the fish smells wafting in the windows and talked of putting all that nationalistic shit behind us. It wasn't us. It wasn't our story. Later, we joined an anarchist feminist group and debated the links between nationalism and patriarchy. A couple of months ago she asked me to marry her. I argued that the institution of marriage was oppressive, but eventually said yes. I won't wear a ring, but she insists on it.

A message pops up on my laptop. It's Maja again. 'Unless you fancy one of the barge bars?'

I type back: 'They wouldn't let me in!'

I catch a tram to Republic Square, where there is a group protesting at Radovan Karadžić's extradition. The protesters are wearing t-shirts with a picture of his face and thick hair that makes him look like Che Guevara. They hold banners that say Free Serbia and Serbia's Last Hero. I stop at the stall selling Karadžić's biography. The wind whips up and people have to fight to hold on to their banners. The stallholder looks me over. 'Where are you from?' he asks in English.

'None of your fucking business,' I reply in Serbian, and walk on. More people are flowing into the square, so I hurry to a side street.

Our 'old haunt' is right in the midst of the fancy cafés and designer shops. The door still doesn't have a sign. Stairs with poster-covered walls lead down to a basement. I find Maja sitting on a stool at the bar. She's the same as her photos: straightened blonde hair and honey tan. She screams when she sees me, 'Seeeennnnnka!'

I find myself laughing and screaming too. Then we're chatting and catching up and she tells me she has her own boutique, which sells designer labels from Spain and Italy. Under her tan and make-up she has the post-thirty lines I have.

'Look at your hair,' she says, and trails off, as if she can't think of anything to say about it. Then she says, 'I'd imagined you in a suit and all grown up in Toronto. But you're... I'd never be brave enough to wear it like that.'

I feel the shaved side of my head. 'Do you want a beer?'

When I get back she asks me questions about Toronto. The club scene. The men. The shops. I drift off. I miss Aida. We could be backpacking together somewhere, jumping on trains to wherever. I'd tell her about the demonstration, and we'd dissect the politics; the nationalism that eats away at people.

'So who's coming down tonight?' I ask.

'Dustan and Ristić.'

'Ristić... *My* Ristić'

'Yeah,' she says, looking into her beer. 'We started seeing each other recently.'

'OK.'

'I hadn't seen him for years, and then I went into a café just off Republic Square. He was working as a waiter. He asked me if I wanted to go for a drink, and I did...'

I nod, not sure what to make of this.

'And you remember Dustan? Your brother's mate.'

'Yeah, he was one of the evacuees, wasn't he?'

We sip our beer. Dustan's uncle whisked him off to Romania to avoid him going to the front. Maja is looking at the group of girls dancing. She shakes her head. 'God, look at the gypos.' They are wearing hot pants and lots of jewellery. The men around the bar are watching them dancing. 'What are they doing in here? I wouldn't serve them in my shop...'

'Do you know what you sound like?'

'What do you mean?' She laughs. 'Anyway, it's only Gypsies.' She sips at her beer, staring at them. 'Still. I wouldn't want an ass like that one.'

I look at her and she says, 'You know it's true!'

I knock back my beer and think about going home as two bald-headed men walk down the stairs.

'It's Dustan and Ristić!' Maja pulls me over to them. It's hard to tell if they are bald or whether they have just shaved their heads; their scalps have a dull sheen under the light. Ristić looks both old and young at the same time. His face is chiselled and hard, and under his t-shirt the lines of his arms are gym-smooth. I imagine him working out all these years, toiling under arm-presses and benches as if working towards enlightenment. He is also looking me up and down. He blinks and frowns, as if he can't place me.

'Ristić, it's Senka.'

'Senka? No way!' He shakes his head, and says to Dustan, 'I'll get this round.'

Dustan is dressed in a black suit, white t-shirt and dark glasses, with a gold cross around his neck. 'Hardly recognised you, Senka. You look amazing. Like G.I. Jane.'

'Thanks... '

Ristić comes back with four shots of šljivovica as well as the beers. He puts them on the table and then leans over to give Maja a long kiss. He runs his hand up her thigh to squeeze her ass, and she slips her arm around his waist. I put my beer down and go to the toilet. Sitting in the stall, my jeans around my knees, I stroke the fine hairs on my thigh and try to remember what it was like going out with Ristić. It was so long ago, I can't really remember. Those long years of the war, while he waited to be conscripted and I planned my escape. Going out, hanging around squares in Belgrade. Groups of teenagers, with the odd bottle of brandy we could get our hands on. Bored out of our minds and just wanting something to happen, but not sure what. When he was conscripted, it was too late; he'd missed most of the action.

Then I remember and shudder, putting my head in my hands. In bed with Ristić – he had sneaked me into his room without his parents knowing – and lying there, the duvet drawn low over my stomach, he looked at my chest, as if he was disappointed at what wasn't there. I pulled up the duvet and he glanced away. I was angry then at the posters on his walls of voluptuous women, though I didn't think about asking him to take them down. I just lay there, and under the cover I slowly ran my hand over my breast, and then got up to go home.

I pull up my jeans and go out to face them again. Maja is at the sink, applying lip liner. 'So how are things going with Ristić?' I ask, washing my hands.

'Great. Just great.'

She is frowning and concentrating on getting a perfect line, so I say, 'Maja. You can do better than him, you know.'

She turns to me, raising her eyebrows. 'Sorry?'

'You are so much better than that.'

She checks her teeth then looks me over, 'Do you think I want to be like you?'

I wipe my hands on my jeans. 'Well if you want to be a doll for some macho dick.'

She puts her lipstick in her handbag and walks out without looking at me. I should probably get out of here. I head out of the toilets and towards the stairway, but Dustan grabs my arm and drags me to where Maja is standing at the bar. 'Now what would these two lovely ladies like to drink?' Neither of us responds so Dustan says, 'Šljivovica for you two then. Peach?' He orders, and then picks up the two shots, puts a suited arm around each of our shoulders, and holds a glass at our lips. 'Right,' he says. 'On three. One. Two. Three. Drink,' and tips the brandy into our mouths. It trickles down both of our chins.

'What a fucking idiot,' Maja says, wiping her face, and laughing. Ristić comes over, saying it's his round. He does the same routine and gets the brandy down both our fronts. We both laugh while he tries to dab Maja's cleavage with his hand. She bats at him and wipes herself. Dustan takes out a pristine handkerchief from his pocket, shakes it dramatically and wipes my neck and shoulders. 'Welcome home,' he says, grinning.

More shots appear and we do them all together, banging our glasses on the counter. Maja seems to have forgotten about our chat in the toilets as she leans against Ristić. He kisses her cheek and brushes her fringe out of her eyes, seeming all loving and kind, and I think of Aida and wonder why she hasn't contacted me.

I turn to Dustan and ask him what he's done over the years.

He says there were no jobs with all the sanctions so he started working for his uncle, dealing currency, but now he's got his own bona fide business in a market. He asks whether I'm into stockings.

'Not really, got any socks?'

'Lots. You should come down to the stall. I'll give you a discount.'

'I might just do that.' We smile at each other and clink glasses. Then the music changes. 'It's Ceca!' Maja cries. 'Come on!'

'No no no!'

'Come on,' she laughs and dances backwards, fluttering her hands in a Ceca-like way. The guitars and violins build up a tempo and Ceca sings her folk-vibrato. Maja grabs my arm, dragging me onto the dance floor. We do ironic sexy dancing, exaggerating Ceca's moves, waving our hands above our heads and singing into pretend microphones. Soon the whole room is dancing to the turbofolk, even Dustan and Ristić. Our arms in the air, singing along and whooping, the four of us dance together, hugging and laughing, and for a moment the years drop away; I remember why I was friends with them.

When the song ends, I get a beer and Maja carries on dancing. Ceca was big in the nineties. When I was going out with Ristić, I wanted a curvy body like hers. Ceca married Arkan, a leader of the Volunteer Guard. Dalivor worshipped Arkan, and now both Dalivor and Arkan are dead, but Ceca is still making music, and we're dancing again to her songs, as if nothing has changed.

Maja leans against the bar next to Ristić, running her hand down his arm. She's watching the Roma girls in the middle of the floor, pulling their tops down and doing moves for the suited men leaning against the bar. One of the girls dances towards a man and grabs hold of his tie, pulling him towards her, then she dances away with her back to him. I think, Maja's right. They shouldn't be in here, and I check my pockets as I stand up.

It's late when I finally get home, drunk and drenched from the rain. I stagger into the study and pick up some of my father's articles. I try to read through one or two, steadying myself against the desk. Lines and phrases pop out:

> The Serbian people have to strive for a full national and cultural integrity without regard for republic or province... Serbs cannot be a minority anywhere or they lose their honour.... Serbs have fought for freedom throughout history. They have been persecuted by fundamentalist Ottomon Turks and they were slaughtered by their Ustaöe neighbours in this century. Self definition is needed or history will repeat itself... we are not taking these territories away from the Bosniaks. They are ethnically Serbian territories.

I laugh. 'Warmong-er-er,' I sing in a Ceca-like warble. 'My father is a warmonger-er-er.' It seems the funniest thing. I dump the articles on the floor, and stagger into the hall, the ceiling spinning and my ears still ringing from the music. I switch the light on and open my father's door. His face is gaunt and his mouth hangs loosely open. My mother is asleep in a chair, her head to the side. She is wrapped in a purple dressing gown and wearing matching fluffy slippers. Those journalists don't understand. Not really. Not the complexity. My father's face twitches, as if a dream is passing through him, and I wonder if he's dreaming about our pasts or what we could have been if war hadn't blighted out lives.

My mother blinks, 'Senka,' she murmurs, reaching over to feel my father's pulse. Satisfied, she sinks back in the chair.

'Senka,' she says again. 'You don't know what it means to have you back.'

Lebensborn

HANNA WAS EXHAUSTED. She had risen at five to take the train from Oslo Central Station to the airport. The plane had been delayed; her face felt puffy and her feet were swelling out of her shoes like cupcakes. No matter how she adjusted her long skirt, she couldn't hide them.

The tall, blonde air stewardess, whose feet Hanna had noticed were also swollen, was holding out a bin bag, so Hanna passed her the empty tray, and turned back to the book. She'd studied the hardback cover and stared at the ridiculous title for what felt like most of the flight. Her mother, Kari, had publicised her life and sold her diary to another sensationalist book, even if it had the veneer of academia: *Horizontal Collaboration: Gender and Politics in Occupied Norway.*

She didn't trust academia. She had her ex-husband to thank for that.

She eased her heel out of her court shoe. It relieved the pinch, but if she took her shoes off completely she'd never get them back on again. The young girl next to her was wearing battered trainers. Kari had probably worn high heels to attract the soldiers. That awful academic, Dr Gunda Overland-Knudsen, had worn red pumps, which had matched her died henna hair. She had been full of condolences at Kari's funeral, but was still clearly annoyed that Hanna had declined to contribute to her parasitical study.

Hanna had stared at the cover long enough. She pushed her glasses up her nose, opened the book till she heard the

35

spine crack and found the section on her mother. She skipped to the photos of the diary, of brown crinkled notepaper and swirly handwriting and then looked at the translated excerpts in English. Here were her mother's words, in bald, black print.

13 May 1944

I met someone today.

The streets of Oslo were packed. Birna and I were at Karl Johan's Gate. There was one of the German parades going by, so we had to stand and cheer. Men crowded in shop doors, some waving their caps, others folding their arms and staring. Some lads didn't wave and got a ticking off from a sergeant on the side of the road. One started arguing with him and was knocked to the ground. I strained to look, but the crowd pressed us towards the front. The music was stirring, almost joyous. I was waving my handkerchief when one of the passing German soldiers swivelled his head, looked straight into my eyes and winked. I jumped. It was as if a marching doll had come to life. Then he was gone, his back disappearing into the rows of brown shirts.

'Did you see that?' I asked.

Later, we were walking home and the soldier appeared on a corner. Perhaps he had followed us. He walked over and said, 'Good afternoon,' in Norwegian, though his pronunciation was terrible. My hands were bare and red from the cold. He offered to take me out and find me some gloves and ten pounds of potatoes. My stomach jumped at the sound of the potatoes. It was probably my stomach answering, my stomach that said yes.

The plane was landing, but Hanna carried on flicking through the book. In another photo with the Norwegian women who had participated in the study, Kari was classically dressed, like a model in an old knitting magazine: straight wool skirt, cashmere cardigan, pearl buttons. Her hair was long and still blonde, just faded with age.

Hanna braced herself for the landing, closing her eyes as the plane jumped on the runway. She peered through the porthole at Manchester Airport's Terminal 1. When she got home she would have to face her daughter.

'What do you mean you knew she was ill?' Mary had screeched, breaking abruptly at the lights. 'She. Had. Cancer. And you didn't say anything? You just ignored it?'

'I didn't ignore it,' Hanna said, pulling her skirt over her knees. 'You don't understand.'

'Don't I? Nothing can compete with your sacrosanct pain, can it?'

At twenty, Hanna had been brave; she had saved up her money for a flight to London, where she'd found a waitressing job and lived in a poky bed and breakfast in Camden that took all her wages. When she walked home in the dead of night, she would stuff her hands in her mac pockets and keep her head down. In her room, she'd perch on the narrow bed, eating soup from a tin. Then, one night, Thomas came into the restaurant with a group of friends. He'd been to the theatre to see Ibsen. When he heard her accent he asked her what she thought of *Hedda Gabler*. She blushed. She'd heard of it, but she hadn't seen it. 'You should,' Thomas said, as he sipped his wine. 'I'll take you.'

That moment had stuck in her mind. Thomas offering to take her, this unknown, foreign waitress, to the theatre in front of his friends; he stood up, as if he was a gallant knight and took the dishes from her arms. His friends thought this was uproarious, but the manager stood tight-lipped as he swept past and dumped them on the nearest surface in the kitchen, and then sauntered back as if he had broken some unspoken rule.

A few months later she moved into a flat with Thomas

and his two friends who were completing their theses. They lived 'in sin' for a year. If sin was a place you inhabited, hers was a dirty flat with brown and orange wallpaper and mice.

'You'll turn out like your mother,' her grandmother had always said. 'Just the same.'

14 May 1944

He took me to Theatercafeen! It was all sumptuous brocade and silver cutlery, although even this restaurant looked a little threadbare. I spruced up for it – hair curled, the last of my lipstick worked into my lips and charcoal darkening my eyebrows. Barend was in his uniform, carrying a bulging satchel which he opened to show me the potatoes. I gasped. It was as though he had given me a bunch of roses, only potatoes were better than roses. Then he got out the gloves and I could have died. They were made of soft cream leather. I put them on, but they were a little too small. I felt like one of Cinderella's ugly sisters and I'd have to cut off my fingers to make them fit. But he didn't seem to notice. He was looking at the menu.

'There's not much to order,' he said. 'We will have the fish soup. You need fattening up.'

We had beer with the soup. It was watery, but strong for me, since I haven't had any in months! I asked him about his home. He said he was from a village in the Black Forest. He had a large family. All his brothers were in the army, and his sisters were left to farm the land. They were very strong and his mother said that they worked better than the boys.

We laughed at this.

Barend is very thin and I could imagine his sisters opening barn doors for him.

He walked me home and left me at the end of my road. Mother was waiting at the window and saw us, but said nothing when I walked into the kitchen.

Hanna buttoned up her coat. A tall blonde couple stood up in the seats in front of her. They had to bend over, their heads brushing the overhead lockers. The woman had the same long blonde hair as Hanna's mother and grandmother. Hanna felt her own, dark bob. Her hair had turned grey at thirty and she'd coloured it ever since. She stood up and squeezed down the aisle behind the couple.

If Hanna had a diary she would have to write, 'I missed my mother's funeral.' When the solicitor had contacted her with the date for Kari's funeral, she wandered through the rooms of her home, looking at the dark wooden furniture and the Laura Ashley decorations as if she had never seen them before, and then she caught a plane to Oslo. Arriving late at night, she crept out of Gardermoen Airport as if she was hiding from someone. The taxi was extortionate, everything in Norway was extortionate. She huddled in the back seat and stared at the passing roads, the people spilling out of bars along Prinsens Gate. She was a stranger here. A tourist. Hanna booked into the first hotel she could find on Rosenkrantz Gate. In her room, she made a vodka from the mini bar. She drank it on the bed with its crisp white sheets and rubbed her aching calves. Then she had another and lay back, thinking she was in for a sleepless night, but in the morning she woke with the light on and her cardigan twisted around her. She got up from the bed feeling stiff and grubby. She showered and changed into a black suit. It made her look tired and the skirt pinched her waist, so she left the button undone.

'Vestre Gruvlund, vær så snill,' she said to the driver, the words awkward and strange on her lips. She was forgetting her own language. 'What's Norwegian for "fridge" mum?' Mary asked once. 'Why won't you speak it? I could be fluent, bilingual, but you won't speak it.'

There were road works on Sorkiedalsvelen, so the taxi drove her to what turned out to be the entrance to the old part of the cemetery. She was late and there was no one to ask for directions. She began to walk towards the graves, as if she was drawn to them, carrying a bunch of carnations she'd bought at the airport. The rows of grey, crumbling headstones spread out before her. She could make out dates: 1939, 1945. Graves that were neglected now, without flowers, the markings faded and covered in moss. Then there were shiny black graves, with gold lettering, and white graves, some yellowed, others a glistening pearl. Amidst them were copses of trees and bushes. From somewhere, was the sound of a digger chugging up earth.

Her grandparents had been cremated and had small plaques in a section near the crematorium, but Kari had opted for the full works.

Another funeral was taking place just ahead. A woman was throwing flowers into the hole, and the group of people were standing in silence. Hanna continued walking along the path. She should find the office and ask someone, but where the hell was it?

She ventured onto the grass, her heels sticking in the earth. She couldn't even see where she had come in. The graves stretched out around her; labyrinthine rows of headstones, some oval, others with crosses and decorations; angels and curving leaves. It seemed, as she turned round and round, looking for the office, that there was nothing in the world but this cemetery; nothing but markers of the dead.

Hanna walked faster, not caring that her shoes were ruined. She realised she was crying, and then she tripped, her knee going into the dirt. She wiped her leg as best she could and let herself cry for a couple of minutes. She wiped her face and carried on walking; more graves and trees, then a path that led to the office. She stumbled inside, out of breath, as if she'd walked for miles.

Placing her hands on the desk, she said to the woman in English, 'I can't find the funeral.'

'Sorry?'

'I can't find my mother's funeral. I don't know where it is. I'm lost.'

'What name?'

'Kari Orheik'

'I think they have finished. But here, I'll take you.'

She drove Hanna in a buggy, like the ones on Thomas' golf course, to where her mother's coffin lay in the ground. The funeral party had gone and Hanna was left to throw the carnations into the hole while the woman waited a few feet away.

18 May1944

I felt delirious walking home. Another soldier called out to me and followed me down the street. I don't know what he said, but I ignored him. It was as if I was surrounded by glass and no one could touch me.

Mother stared at me as if it was stamped on my forehead. She circled me in the kitchen, eyeing me up and down. 'Where have you been?'

'Nowhere.'

She got a cloth and grabbed me by the neck, rubbing it across my face. Then she dragged me to the sink and scrubbed my lips with a brush.

'You've been with him, haven't you? That German soldier. You know what they'll call you? A Nazi's whore.'

I am writing this in the dark, feeling the page with my hands. My lips are raw and bleeding.

Birna is snoring across the room. Loud, raucous snores, as if she is laughing in her sleep. She'd tiptoed round the kitchen when all this was going on, tidying, wiping her hands on her pinny; doing her impression of a good daughter.

Today, we didn't go for lunch. He took me to a hotel room, where bread, ham and beer were laid out on the dressing table. The bread was reflected in the mirror and behind it was me, pale with red lips. There was ice on the windows and the room was even colder than my room at home. The bedcover looked clean, so I supposed that was a good thing.

Next to the ham he placed a packet of stockings. I

gasped and then covered my mouth, as if I'd hiccupped. Picking them up, I said, 'They're beautiful.' The stockings were so exquisite I could hardly touch them. I folded my arms across my chest to keep warm and he poured the beer. Really, I wanted tea, something hot in a steamy café where there wasn't a neatly made bed. I drank the beer and we nibbled the bread.

He said my hair was pure, as if it was light itself.

I laughed as he pulled out a strand and held it up.

'You are a goddess,' he said. 'Perfect.'

He wanted to know about my family. Who were my grandparents, even my great-grandparents? Were they all Norwegian? What did they look like? Were they tall and blonde like me?

I said they were purely Norwegian. Were his family all German?

Of course they were. He had pure German blood.

He ran his finger along my jaw and down my neck. Then he undid the top button of my blouse and stroked my collarbone. His mouth was slightly open and I thought he was going to kiss me, but he ran his hand down my arm to my hand and led me to the bed.

He sat on the edge and I stood before him. I stayed perfectly still as he unbuttoned my blouse and unzipped my skirt. Then he slipped off my underskirt and I shivered.

He smiled up at me, and his smile was so open and sweet; I thought how young he was, as young as me. We were just children.

'You're shivering,' he said. So I undid my boots and slid under the cold sheet.

At passport control, Hanna took out her Norwegian and British passports, but then handed over the British one, in which her name was Hanna Johnson and she wasn't a visitor; she belonged. The man in the booth hardly glanced at it and sent her through.

Tyskerunger. Naziyngel.

'Naziyngel,' Hanna muttered. She'd not forgotten those words. They were spat at her in the playground. *Nazi spawn.*

At baggage collection, passengers grabbed the suitcases sailing past on the belt. She couldn't remember what hers looked like. Was it brown or beige?

Naziyngel. And Thomas wondered why she had what he called a 'persecution complex.'

Hanna switched her phone on, but Mary hadn't texted. 5pm. She'd be getting home from school, tired and cranky.

Hanna had made sure that Mary hadn't heard those words or grown up with the shame. Mary had wanted to come to the funeral. She'd pulled her long blonde hair back and said in her teacher voice, 'I'll come with you.'

'No, I'm better on my own.'

'She's *my* grandmother.'

Mary had inherited her grandmother's good looks and height. At thirteen she was already five foot ten and Hanna found it difficult to hug such an overgrown daughter. Since Hanna's divorce Mary had turned into a bossy madam. 'Mum, why don't you join the singles bingo club? Here's an advert for art classes.' Hanna looked through the leaflets and placed them on the table; there was no remedy for waking in the night, panicking because the duvet was flat and neat where it should have been rumpled and full of Thomas.

There was her case coming round the bend.

No one else from the family had come to Kari's funeral. Hanna had caught another overpriced taxi from the cemetery to the nearby hotel, and edged into the specially reserved back room.

The other mourners were mostly women like Kari, going by their height, blondeness and age. They were standing in groups by the bar, sipping glasses of white wine. The women and men of Hanna's age who were sitting at the tables were obviously the Lebensborn.

Hanna took a glass of wine from the bar and sat at an empty table. She felt short and frumpy next to everybody. If the Lebensborn thing had worked, she would have been a failure.

The academic woman, Gunda Overland-Knudsen, strode over, her bracelets jingling. She was even shorter than Hanna, and flopped herself onto a chair. 'You're Kari's daughter!' she exclaimed. 'I knew you were when you came in.'

Hanna smiled and sipped her wine.

'This is for you.' Gunda placed a copy of the book on the table.

'Thank you.'

Gunda asked her about her trip over, how she was doing in the UK. Hanna said that she had recently retired from her job in the department store. And then they talked about Kari. The last time Gunda had seen her a few weeks ago you wouldn't have known how ill she was. Gunda sipped her white wine. 'Have you applied for compensation?' she asked.

'No.' Hanna said. 'I don't think that's for me.'

'Oh, but you should.'

Thinking of it irritated Hanna even now. Gunda had acted as if it was a book launch, not a funeral.

As Hanna's beige suitcase reached her, she heaved it off the belt and onto the floor. The shrill of the alarm made her jump. People around her paused. Perhaps it would stop in a moment. But it didn't. The belt came to a halt and passengers shoved past each other to reach their stranded bags.

'What about my bags?' a suited man said to those around him. 'How am I going to get my bag now?'

Hanna extended the suitcase handle and dragged it towards customs. As passengers rushed to the exit, they pushed past and someone knocked the handle from her grasp. She had to fight against the tide of people to retrieve it.

1 August1944

This morning, Mother stood in the kitchen and asked if she had raised me for this? From the doorway Father shouted, 'To be an enemy to Norway?' He strode over and raised his hand, but Mother said, 'Don't. Not in her condition.'

'What does that matter?' he said.

'Kari. The Germans are here now. But what about the future? The only thing we can do is hope they lose, and you go making your bed with one.'

'I'm not an enemy of Norway,' I said. 'Neither is Barend.'

'Don't you dare use that name in this house.'

I ran upstairs to my room and lay on my bed.

15 August 1944

I'm not allowed out now I'm showing. Mother says it's too dangerous. I stay in my room, watching the street from my window. I think about Barend and wonder if I know him at all. But then I imagine him kissing me and how he'd tried to pick me up to carry me across the hotel room, but I was too tall and he stumbled and we fell onto the bed. I think about how I like to place my hand on his chest, run it over his jacket and shirt and then undo a couple of buttons and slip my hand inside to feel the muscle and wiry hairs. Then I unbutton his shirt and he leans over, his whole body going taut.

I don't know him really. Perhaps it's because we never understand each other! His Norwegian is poor and my German is terrible. When I speak in German he says my accent makes me sound adorable, like a little girl.

1 September 1944

Barend came to the house late at night and asked to see me. My parents didn't want to let him in, but he said he would bring officers. I am being rescued. He is my St Hallvard! I just hope we don't die together. I was in my nightgown, so I quickly dressed and came downstairs. He said he was worried about me and that I should go into a special maternity hospital. I'd get the best care. He said there was even fresh fruit for me to eat. So I packed a small suitcase. He is coming tomorrow to get me.

Outside the Terminal, Hanna had to walk to the roundabout to find a taxi. Others had the same idea; there was a trail of people, talking on phones and dragging suitcases. When a taxi finally stopped at the roundabout a woman asked if anyone wanted to share it. Five people fitted in, and Hanna sat in the front. The passengers complained about losing their luggage; that it was still on the carousel; who knew how they'd get it back. Hanna turned to look at the airport. Everything seemed normal, apart from the smoke rising from one of the buildings behind it.

15 November 1944

We have to eat toast and porridge for breakfast. The nurses say it's Himmler's orders. How strange a big general worrying about what we have for breakfast!

The maternity home is a converted manor house, where rich people once lived. It's like a very clean hotel, all crisp and neat and white, as if the germs have been ordered to stay at the door, where the soldiers wipe their boots.

I have my own room. I can see other girls and hear them walking down the corridor, but we are not encouraged to talk to each other. Though we are all here for the same reason, we are alone and solitary. This morning I tried tapping on my wall, but laughed at myself and gave up.

Barend comes to see me every day. He brings fruit, flowers and little bars of chocolate. He said he'd bring me cigarettes but he isn't allowed. He is very proud, as if he has accomplished something great. He patted my stomach, which is huge now, asking, 'How is the Reich's child? How is our Lebensborn?'

I asked him what Lebensborn was.

'Born free,' he said. 'In the New World.'

'I want to go home.'

'But you're safe here. You'll get the best treatment.'

'Do you love me?'

'Of course I do.'

I told him I wanted to go home and began to cry.

'You must have the baby here. Do you understand?'

A nurse gave me a tablet and when I woke in the night, I felt hazy, so I slept till I didn't know what day it was. Hanna was the last in the taxi. It had dropped the others off in Didsbury and the city centre before driving down the Crescent, past the University where Thomas used to work, to Irlams o'th' Height. The taxi turned off Bolton Road onto King's Road. She felt the judder of the speed bumps and looked to see if the Height library was still open. Then they turned onto Godfrey Road, with its familiar detached houses. 'Just here is fine,' she said to the driver.

'Thirty quid,' he said.

She had a handful of money from everybody. It was more than that, so she gave it all to him.

She dashed into the house. Letters and newspapers were piled behind the door. Bills, and some junk mail for Thomas, which she stuffed into the 'Thomas's letters' box. Seeing his name still made her pause, even after two years.

The house had a funny, unlived-in smell, though she had only been away for three days. She hurried through to the living room, and turned on the TV. The BBC news channel was reporting from the airport, saying a fire had closed all runways.

She should call Mary. But all her energy seemed to have left her. She lay back on the couch and closed her eyes. Then she shook off her shoes and sat up to reach for her bag.

1 December 1944

They brought the baby. It had a shock of dark hair and a red screwed–up face.

'That's not mine.'

The nurse put it into a cot, saying, 'I'm afraid you'll have to leave.'

'It's not mine. Look at its hair. Where... where's Barend?' I asked. But she didn't answer. I was told I had to go home and to take my child with me. I kept saying it wasn't mine, but they wouldn't listen.

I was still weak and sore, but I dressed and walked like a crab. I had to carry the baby out of the hospital in my arms. She cried and cried. It was a long way home and I had to rest on the road.

Mother and Father were in the kitchen. They said nothing. But then Birna came over and stared at the baby. I dumped it in her arms and struggled upstairs.

'Isn't it blonde enough for them?' Father shouted.

8 May 1945

The allies have arrived and the Germans are fleeing. The neighbours are celebrating in the street, waving the Norwegian flag and dancing around. Mother took down the blackout paper. I hid from the window. I should feel glad, but I don't.

I don't know what has happened to Barend. Other soldiers walked out of buildings with their hands in the air apparently. Many are going back on boats. Will he contact me now? Can he?

A few weeks ago there was a news broadcast from the Norwegian government in Britain, warning against collaboration. The broadcaster said something about women who had not shown restraint, but Mother switched it off.

There is a change in the air. Everybody is cursing the Germans.

The same information kept being repeated on the news, so Hanna switched it off, and read over and over the words describing her.

The baby is thin and weak... There is nothing to feed her... Now the war is over, I hope there will be milk. You'd think that Kari's sister would be Hanna's surrogate mother, but she got married a few months later, and that was the last of her attention.

I hope Barend escaped on a boat.

Hanna had asked Gunda at the funeral about what had happened to her father. They had been nibbling pieces of rye bread with herring.

'I looked into it for Kari,' Gunda had said. 'She wanted to know after all these years. I believe he didn't make it home but I can't be sure. Many of the retreating German ships were bombed.'

Hanna looked around her living room for some paper. There was a notebook and biro beside the phone. The notebook was small, but it would do. She opened a page and thought about what she'd write about her childhood. She remembered the long corridor in the children's home, and reaching up to run her hand along the rail; the baby dolls in the day room, which she and the other girls took turns playing with. And then she next remembered an old lady turning up one day at the home, saying she was her grandmother and Hanna would live with her now.

She closed the notebook. It was no good. It was too long ago now. She did not know how to write it. That silly woman's academic book was everything she had. She picked it up again and turned to her mother's last entry.

15 May 1945

I was washing sheets when they came. Mother answered the door and asked what they wanted.

They didn't reply. The door banged as they threw it back and barged inside. I remained where I was, scrubbing a sheet in soapy water. They pushed themselves into the kitchen: amongst them a married couple from our road and the man who owned a local shop.

'Kari Orheik,' one of them said.

'I saw her going about with one of them,' the woman from our road said, grabbing my arm. She looked into my eyes, satisfied. 'German whore.'

A truck was waiting out the front. Inside, women were huddled on the floor. Their clothes were torn and one was crying. I was pushed inside. I sat and hugged my knees. The sickness I had felt ever since the war had ended, and the allies had retaken Oslo, built up in my stomach and I thought I was going to vomit. 'Where are we going?' I asked. One shrugged. A small, pale girl said, 'I don't know.' One had bruises on her face, her cheek a deep purple. They stopped and more girls were forced into the truck. One was heavily pregnant and lay down on the floor.

We drove in silence, swaying as the truck turned corners. I thought of St Hallvard, and how he might come to rescue girls like us, like he had the woman who had boarded his ship, but he and the woman had died anyway. And this thought, that they had died anyway, frightened me more than anything.

Eventually, the truck stopped and the doors opened. 'Get out,' a man said. We stood up and climbed out. The pregnant girl struggled. We had to help her; the man just stood and watched.

We were at Karl Johan's Gate. The Nazi flags had been torn down, but it was as full as when there had been the German parades. People gathered around us. Old women, mothers with children, young men and a couple of boys I knew from school. One boy pushed to the front and stared at me. German whore, he mouthed. Faces as far back as I could see, their arms raised, shouting, shouting.

'Tyskertøser!'

The policeman ordered them back, but they kept on chanting and pushing towards us. The pregnant girl was on the ground. Another girl tried to pick her up, but she was hauled off by a man in the crowd. I found myself cradling the girl next to me. She was crying, but the rest of us were silent. We huddled together, arms around each other, as the crowd chanted, Tyskertøser!

Someone set a German flag alight in front of us and I couldn't breathe from the smoke. And then I couldn't hear what they were shouting anymore; I could only see them pushing in as they began to pinch and grab my arms, and a woman tried to pull my hair, and everything went silent and black.

Hanna put the book down. She was shivering so she knelt at the fireplace and piled paper and wood into the grate. She lit the edges of the paper and waited for the kindling to spread to the wood. There had been a wave of silence running through the family, lapping around them, around the shame. She hadn't wanted Mary to feel it, but she had.

When the fire began to crackle she got up to close the curtains. Outside, it was still light. The grass needed mowing. Her roses had flowered, their heads wide and heavy with maroon petals. She paused with the curtain in her hand and watched two young men sauntering past. Youths like that frightened her. The older one dragged his hand through her roses, sending the petals flying. He turned his shaved head, his blue eyes catching hers as he put up his finger, mouthing, 'Fuck you.' She jumped back, but as he walked on, she gave him the same gesture.

She laughed, letting go of the curtain. Hanna putting up a finger at a youth. She was tougher than she thought.

My Sangar

It was a while ago now, when it was anchored on the hilltop; that green-plated scaffold. I tell you, it hurts my eyes.

In the evenings, the red light slipped through the curtains and into my kitchen. They say if you don't have anything to hide? And I didn't, but I could always see the tower up on Glassdrummond. I could hear them listening on the phone, watching while I cleared the table and washed the dishes.

One evening, I was making myself a sandwich, and the light still shone across my table, so I picked up my breadbin and took it to the window and slid open its cover. There: just some soda farls, a brown loaf. But that wouldn't satisfy them, so I opened my press doors: look, some sugar and Barry's tea. I showed them the bone china: the Royal Doulton cups and saucers. I'm sure they liked those. They're English, aren't they?

In my bedroom I gave them a look in the bedding box – it's been in the family longer than the border's been there. See, I pointed with my hand: cream cotton sheets; they were a wedding gift. Beautifully ironed and smelling of the lavender soaps I'd hidden between the folds. I held the soap to the window, as if in offering.

I displayed the contents of my wardrobe: the bakery uniform: blue pinny and blouse, my husband's old Post Office shirt. And then I had an idea. I waved my white nightie on the end of a mop, like a white flag. Surely this was a signal they'd understand.

And my rosary beads, I wasn't hiding those. They were hung in the window.

They sent two of them round to complain, in their camouflage outfits, with berets instead of helmets.

I said good morning, and asked them if they were having a nice stay. Wasn't the weather glorious? One coughed and told me to stop exhibiting myself, and I said wasn't that what they wanted?

They clearly hadn't understood my message. That night, I could see them from the garden, up there, like gods, crouched on the hilltop. So I placed a few things on the lawn. I tell you, it was a beautiful job to do in moonlight and infrared.

I brought a photo of an aborted calf, and one of the car that had crashed into the bollards, and a branch burnt by the emissions. I laid them out on the grass, and in the middle I placed a photo of my husband with the tributes laid where he'd been shot: the cards and flowers, and his name in carnations. I placed them all on the lawn, and the red light flashed over and around them, prodding them, and still they would not see.

Her Blue Shadow

BLUE FLICKERED ON the horizon, as if a stream ran between the rounded peaks of Shekarvar Ghar, but the blue wasn't water, it was a cloth flapping in the wind; the silk of Leila's chadari, the blue painted around her eyes. She had been so beautiful on their wedding night.

The blue turned to white in the afternoon sun. Bashir rubbed his eyes; they hurt from studying the range, but he had seen nothing, no one all day. Just the endless sandy rocks and sloping mountains, while Abdul smoked and Bashir tried not to think of anything.

Bashir and Abdul had spent the winter months in the network of caves and bunkers left over from the Soviet war. The caves were extensive, but not as complex as the ones in Tora Bora. Four or five had been reinforced and had thick metal doors. In the corners, there were relics of old transistor radios and empty shells.

Bashir had stammered when he met Abdul – a mujahideen hero come to life, who had fought for fifteen years in the Hindu Kush. But he didn't know the terrain like Abdul; he was a Barakzai from Kandahar and until a few months ago, he'd never held a gun or climbed a mountain. Abdul seemed to have been made from a mountain, as if he had been born in one, and when conflict came, he was cut out of the rock. He didn't even have any scars. Perhaps the wilderness had protected him. When Bashir said this, Abdul laughed. 'It is Allah who preserves my beauty.' He pulled at the edges of his eyes and stretched out the wrinkles. Bashir blinked at him. 'You Taliban,' Abdul said. 'You are too serious.'

Outside the cave entrance, the temperature was dropping as dusk drew in. Abdul was sitting on a nearby rock, relighting his old-fashioned chillum, while Bashir squeezed the pieces of paper folded in his hand.

'You should hurry up,' Bashir said. 'It's changeover.'

'Here. Have some then.'

He shook his head. It was forbidden, but Abdul got away with things like that. After all, he had fought alongside Mullah Mohammad Omah himself in Sangesar as well as in the assault on Kandahar airport that had driven the Russians out.

At that time, Bashir had been a child, living in a refugee camp in Panjpai. His uncles had stayed to fight and were martyred, while his father had taken the extended family to safety. They shared the camp with thousands of refugees, as well as scorpions and spiders that scuttled out of the tents when you shone a light in them. After they were married, Leila told him that she was born in that camp, and that she kept a scorpion called Saleh in a box, which she used to scare her brothers.

The sun was burning amber over the mountains, and to his right, the cave entrance was hidden by overhanging rocks. The replacements were climbing towards them. They were young with patchy beards they were obviously desperate to grow. Bashir reported that there had been nothing of note, while Abdul blew out his chillum, so they could go inside. At the entrance, there were two more guards and greetings. They shone their torches into the cave and made their way to the back wall where there was a tunnel. Even now, when he entered, it felt like walking into a tomb, as if the walls were closing in on him; the tunnel narrowed till it was less than a metre high and they had to crawl through the hole, their shoulders brushing the crystalline walls, till it opened into a wider cavern. The mullahs had their own built-up bunker at the back, while the rest of them slept on the cold floor. There were about thirty men huddled against stoves, warming their hands. Many were Noorzai, and some had come from Pakistan. Bashir was the only Barakzai there.

Bashir and Abdul joined the others in the final prayers of the day. Then Abdul lay down, pulled his blanket around him and fell asleep.

Leila had married Bashir three years ago. Her family was from the Daman district of Kandahar, and he had caught glimpses of her through a doorway at his cousin's wedding – a delicate hand, eyes like bowls – so he'd asked his mother to approach her family, and they immediately said yes. Leila came to live with him and his family in the city centre, where they owned a factory that made prosthetic limbs and wheelchairs. When she arrived she seemed pleased with their room; she placed her jewellery box on the low table and folded her clothes next to his. She took off her veil, and stared straight ahead, her eyes bright with blue shadow. Bashir stood next to her and stroked her beautiful, thick hair.

'Can I brush it?'

She didn't respond so he got a comb and began to brush the long pony tail. After a while she smiled, undid her clips and let her hair fall down her back.

Every evening she would say, 'Bashir, do my hair.'

So this became their game: he was her hairdresser. He'd style her hair from photos in *Marie Claire* and *Cosmopolitan*, which his mother had kept hidden for years alongside *Time Magazine* and *The National Geographic*. The hairstyles were just for him. He'd pin her hair on top of her head, with tendrils hanging down. One time, he cut a thick fringe, which fell over her eyes. Then he'd pretend that she was a princess and he her servant; he'd bow and bring her pomegranates and grapes.

When Leila became pregnant a few months later, she

didn't want him to do her hair anymore. He remembered them lying together on the bed, listening to the distant gunfire, the drone of airplanes and Leila asking, 'Why do they presume they can come here?'

'Don't think about it. Just think of the baby,' he murmured, stroking her stomach.

She turned on her side, picking up *Time Magazine*. 'I have to think about it.'

He peered over her shoulder, seeing a photograph of a bald man sitting on the ground. 'What are you looking at?'

'Nothing,' she said, closing the magazine.

Bashir wrapped his patu around him. The other men lay close together for warmth, sharing blankets and pillows, but Abdul kept his heat to himself. The uneven wall of the cave was damp on Bashir's back and he could hear the sound of dripping water. There were mats on the ground, but these were damp too. He had already begun to shiver.

'She locked me in here.'

He could hear her words, hot and breathy in his ear. Leila was crouched next to him, grasping his arm. She wasn't wearing her chadari, even though the cave was full of men. She was dressed as if at home. 'Please,' she whispered. 'She locked me in here.'

The lamps were blown out and he pulled his patu over his head. Beside him there was a groan. Abdul. A comforting sound. But still, he could feel her nails digging into his arm.

In the morning, they prayed and then ate flatbread while the Mullah told the group that half of them would stay and the other half would be leaving by seven. Bashir, Abdul and others walked down the stony path to where it joined a dirt trail. Here, nothing grew apart from a ragged kind of moss that even goats could not chew.

They walked till they reached a small mountain village, where they stayed with a family who were kind, and tried to give them the last of their bread, but the Mullah said they would eat nothing, not when the children were so thin. In the morning, they marched down to Ghorak Valley, where there was a dirt track and four cars were waiting. Two of them joined each car and the others continued walking. It would take them a day by car to get to the town.

Bashir was in a car with Abdul, Farzan, and a driver. He kept his eyes on the dusty planes and the grey and brown mountains beyond, thinking that Kandahar was on the other side of them. Soon the mountains were in the distance, and they bumped over the track, avoiding the town of Ghorak itself because of the foreign strongholds there. They stopped at nightfall and set off again the next morning. It was after midday when they approached Tansin.

Outside Tansin, the field's crops had been flattened, ridged with tractor lines, their poppies lying crushed and mangled. The mud houses on the outskirts of the village seemed empty. The doors were blasted open. Stones and clumps of mud lay on the ground. They drove into the town, where children watched their car from the roadside, and heads popped up from rooftops. The driver pointed out of the window, saying, 'This was done by a drone. Over there, a smart bomb.' What were once buildings made of breeze blocks were blackened. A compound of houses was blasted open. Rubble, holes, and teetering walls, their stones curving at impossible angles.

They pulled into the bazaar and unloaded their bags from the car. Bashir looked round at the stalls of almonds and pomegranates. He had always loved bazaars: the crush and bustle of people, leading Leila through the crowd. She'd point to what she wanted; it was hard to hear her through the grill. Dates. Chickpeas. Almonds. 'No, not those,' she'd say, gesturing to another sack of almonds. 'Those. They're better.' And he'd barter, never letting go of her hand.

He followed the men through the bazaar and into a compound. The mullah was sitting with the older men of the town, while they talked and ate together.

Bashir and the others took their bags and supplies through a doorway into another room. They unpacked the ammonium nitrate, the cans, and electrical equipment. Two of them, Khalid and Hakim, were experts on explosives, and were cosseted like women in the back room of the compound.

They prepared enough explosives for each car. Bashir enjoyed the bustle and action before missions; it was like the excitement of women preparing for a wedding or a feast.

'Come with us,' his mother had said. She had been packing pots and pans into a box and Rasul was crawling around the kitchen floor. 'Your cousin might be able to get you a position in the civil service. What will you live on here?'

Bashir shook his head.

'I can't make your father give you money. He won't,' she whispered, glancing through the door to where his father was pacing in the other room.

'I don't want anything off you,' he snapped.

'You can't stay here. The city's not safe...'

He leant over his mother, so she shrank back against the table. 'I just want you to go,' he snarled, spit landing on her face.

She started to cry, covering her mouth with her hands. 'How can you say that?'

'It was because of you.'

She stood upright, so he had to step out of the way. 'It wasn't my fault. There was something wrong with her.'

'You're a liar.'

He picked up Rasul and carried him outside to sit on the courtyard steps. His mother wept and banged pans about, as if they were the cause of everything.

But Rasul was a comfort; always happy to be cuddled and thrown in the air. Bashir's family could go and squeeze themselves ten to a room in their cousin's apartment if they wanted. Their prosthetics factory had closed and his father - always ready for a business opportunity - was opening another factory financed by the Red Cross in Kabul.

His grandfather had had a prosperous business in handicraft and carpentry before he started making wooden legs in the seventies. They still had some of those original models, which were beautifully carved and made to order. Prosthetics had come into its own in the camps of Pakistan. His father and grandfather carved wooden legs and sold them to the other refugees. The size of feet, ankles and calves was discussed over every meal. 'Do you know,' his grandfather would say, 'the body can be found in the strangest of shapes.' As children grew, they returned for longer, bigger, wooden legs. In the nineties, when the family had returned to Kandahar, the carpenter's shop grew into a factory and they started making walking sticks and wheelchairs and working in plastic.

Rasul was fidgeting, but Bashir held onto him. The wriggling turned to crying till the noise of a helicopter made them look up at it circling high above. Bashir could almost make out the soldiers inside.

A couple of days later, his family left with Rasul. When they had gone, Bashir searched through the storage room. He unpacked Leila's clothes and gold bracelets. Under them he found torn out pages of magazines: pictures of hairstyles as well as the photo of the bald man. These he looked at, folded and put in his pocket. He picked up the pot of blue eye shadow, which Leila's mother had kept hidden and given to her on their wedding day. He carefully twisted open the lid. The powder had clumped together, but it was still a bright, iridescent blue. He dabbed it on his hand and the colour was so painful that he smeared it over his face, and then he kneeled in the yard. He knew where his path lay.

He dipped his head in water till the blue was washed away and then he left Kandahar by the backstreets, avoiding the roadblocks and ISAF soldiers, and found the mullahs on the outskirts of the city in an abandoned warehouse.

He had presumed the mullahs would be old, but they weren't that much older than him. Mullah Malawi Sadiq nodded when Bashir explained that he was ready to fight. They – the invaders, the foreigners – were a swarm of locusts, flying here, infesting and destroying their country. He would do this for every man, woman and child who had been martyred.

Mullah Malawi Sadiq embraced him. 'Yes, for everyone who has been martyred.'

'For everyone.'

Bashir waited while Khalid and Hasin prepared the explosives for their car. Abdul muttered that he hadn't fought all his life to become a taxi driver, who sneaked around at night, digging holes in roads. Bashir ignored him, helping Khalid close the bonnet of the blue Chevrolet, which was nearly brown with dust. He had completed five successful missions, after watching training videos from Iraq. They had had to guess the translation of the Arabic voiceover, but even so, he had become skilled at planting explosives, with his carpenter's gentle but sure touch.

Abdul drove slowly with the headlights switched off and the windows closed. Soon the car filled with smoke from his chillum. Beneath his turban, Abdul's forehead was creased as he inhaled.

'Are you OK?' Bashir asked.

'Only those in Paradise are OK.'

Bashir turned the photos in his hand. 'I don't want to be in Paradise.'

'You will not find peace, doing this,' Abdul said, gesturing to the back of the car with his chillum.

Bashir wiped at the glass. He couldn't make out much, just the distant shadow of mountains against the moonlight.

Leila appeared in the window: the line of her cheek, her hand touching the pane.

He blinked. But she was still there, her nail broken and bleeding.

He had returned from the factory to find her lying on the bedroom floor. She lifted her head and then put her hands over her face.

'Leila,' he said. Her hair was matted at the back as if she hadn't brushed it. 'Leila.' He knelt down beside her. 'What is it?'

'She locked me in here.'

'What do you mean?'

'Your mother.'

He sat back on his heels. 'Why don't you sit up? I'll get you some water.'

'I don't want any water.'

'What happened?'

She started scratching at the floor with her nail.

'Leila, what happened?'

'I told you. She locked me in here.'

'Leila, you need to try harder. Mother is demanding, but she just wants things to be right.'

She carried on scratching with her finger.

'Stop it. Leila, stop it.' He grabbed hold of her hand. The nail had come partly away; the flesh beneath was raw and bleeding.

'Leila...'

He stared down at her and then went into the kitchen. His mother was sitting on the floor, chopping vegetables.

'What happened?'

She stood up to face him. 'If she won't do any work, she can stay in her room. I'm the one who has to care for her husband and child...'

'I'm not getting involved in your disputes. It's your business.'

'Isn't it your business where she goes in the afternoons? Ask her where she has been. One of the neighbours saw her near the Americans!'

He walked into the courtyard. He could see why his father always worked till dinner was overcooked, and then fell asleep afterwards.

Bashir had no idea how Abdul was navigating without lights. He coughed in the smoke, then unfolded and folded the ripped pages of the magazine. He hadn't asked Leila where she'd been in the afternoons or about the soldiers. He hadn't demanded to know what was going on. Now it was too dark to see the pictures of the hairstyles; too dark to see the black and white photo of a bald man sitting on the ground, while flames billowed out of him.

He wound down the window and threw the pages out. In a second they had disappeared into the darkness. Then he reached for Abdul's chillum and breathed in the smoke.

'You are like my son,' Abdul said, as Bashir stroked the smooth edge of the pipe. He rested his head on the seat; he was filled with softness as if Leila was in the car with them, kissing his neck and cheek.

They had reached the perimeter of the town, where the outskirts met with Zirku. Abdul parked near to a wall. They got out and carried the explosives to the edge of the road. The air was cool, but Bashir was already sweating. By flashlight, he could see the stone wall and the road ahead. He felt the stones, pulled one out, and then another. Abdul dug a hole for the plate and buried the wire in the sand. They placed the canister in the wall and attached the wires. The stones fitted around it.

He stood back to flash his light around while Abdul covered the wires with dirt. They were both gasping for breath and Bashir was drenched in sweat.

There, it was all done. He swung the flashlight over the ground and walked back towards the car.

When he came to, he thought he was on his bed in Kandahar with Leila lying across him. That was her arm and her leg over his. Her weight was heavy and he needed to get her off him.

It was dark, but above him were stars. He was on the ground, covered in gravel and rocks. He couldn't feel any pain, but perhaps that would come. He pushed back his arms and tried to sit up, but something was on him. His face was wet and his lips tasted of blood. 'Abdul,' he said, coughing.

He fell back on the ground, sick and dizzy.

That next evening he had returned home but Leila wasn't there. His parents were in the kitchen. His mother wasn't cooking or doing anything at all. She was crying, 'How could she do this? How could she do this?' His father was standing with his hands at his sides, shaking his head as if he didn't understand.

'Well?' he said to his mother.

'She's at the hospital.'

'What do you mean? Why's she at the hospital?'

'My son...' his father said, reaching to place his hands on Bashir's shoulders, but Bashir turned away.

'Go and see,' his mother said. 'Go and see for yourself what she's done.'

He pulled himself up. He was a few feet from the blast.

'Abdul.' As his eyes got used to the dark he could see rubble strewn on the ground and a shape half covered in rocks. He kicked something soft off him and crawled over. The ground was wet and jagged edges pierced his palms. He touched Abdul's side, the firmness of his chest under his patu; the roundness of his shoulder. 'Abdul,' he whispered. Then he felt the splintered edge of bone and slippery flesh. He expected Abdul to cry out, but he didn't. Bashir knelt over him. Abdul's beard was thick with gravel and his teeth were white and even in the moonlight. But where there should have been his eyes and forehead was crushed, caved in; a mash of hair and bone, grey flesh and blood spread out across the road. His black turban was a couple of feet away, partly unravelled as if Abdul had removed it to protect it from the blast.

'Abdul,' he said again. Then he crawled over to the turban. He tried to wrap it around Abdul's head, but the flattened flesh and bone came away in his hands. Somehow he needed to get the turban back on. He gathered it, wound it in and placed it so it fitted onto the concave of Abdul's forehead.

He stood up and staggered to the side, tripping over the rocks. His head was thick with pain. He walked down the road and across a poppy field. He felt his way around a compound and kept on walking and stumbling.

Bashir had driven his father's car to Mirwais hospital, beeping at the cars in his way. When a van turned in front of him, he leaned out the window and screamed at it. At the hospital, he pushed through the queues of people to the women's ward, which was crammed with beds: burn and blast victims; amputees and pregnancies. He walked down the ward till a doctor touched him on the arm.

'I'm here for Leila Haleem.'

The doctor led him to the corner bed. White gauze covered Leila's right cheek, neck and chest, and the left side of her body. They must have shaved her hair off because the gauze was wrapped around her head.

'A case of self-immolation,' the doctor said, as if Bashir was another doctor and not her husband. 'See. The right hand is not burnt. It rarely is in these cases. There are various full thickness burns of the subcutaneous tissue. Seventy percent of the body. The prognosis isn't hopeful.'

Bashir nodded, though he didn't know what the words meant.

'Apparently, she self-immolated in front of the army base out at the airport.' The doctor lowered his voice. 'They usually do it at home and pretend they caught fire on the stove. Anyway, you will need to purchase more morphine and antibiotics from the pharmacy across the road.'

'Yes, however much she needs.'

He went to the pharmacy and bought what the doctor had ordered. Then he returned and knelt down beside her, his knees hurting on the hard floor. He held her non-burnt hand, and rubbed her soft palm with his thumb. Her lips were cracked and raw and there was a sponge in a cup of water on the bedside table, so he squeezed it into her mouth. She moaned and tried to move her lips. He called for the doctor, who gave her an injection. She quietened and Bashir went to sit on the entrance steps where he watched the patrolling ISAF soldiers and the small boys following them.

Bashir was still walking around the edge of the town. To his left, the fields were dead, and on his right he could make out the walls of another compound. In the distance there was a light, so he headed towards it. In his mind he could see the photo of the burning man, but he understood that the man was Leila; she was this man and she was the blue at the centre of the flame.

In front of Bashir was a tower from which a white light swooped over him, as if inspecting what he was. Voices shouted, shots fired in the air and the white glare came to rest on his face. His legs gave way; he fell to his knees, his hands sinking into the dirt. He couldn't understand the voices and the light was blinding, but as he looked up at the soldiers in front of him, he could see that everything beautiful in the world was blue: the sea, the sky and the shadows between mountains.

The War Tour

I MET AIDA last summer on a ten-hour train ride from Budapest to Sarajevo. I was inter-railing with James, who I'd been seeing for six months. He had recently finished his PhD in critical theory and used words like 'discourse' and 'ideology' in everyday conversation. I wanted to become a journalist, but so far had only written reviews for <u>Manchester. net</u>.

James and I boarded the air-conditioned train in Budapest, but after an hour or so we were shifted onto a coach and then an old fashioned train with six-seat compartments and windows that barely opened.

As the train travelled south, the carriage thickened with heat. My back was damp and my legs stuck to the seat. James had fallen asleep, his head to the side and his brown fringe slick with sweat. I was glad; I could relax. We'd spent the last few days bickering about money and directions, and he'd gone in a mood every time I wanted a quiet moment to do some writing.

We'd taken the window seats, while three Australian lads had slumped in the other corner, their faces glazed and reddened. The girl next to me had short black hair with a long fringe that feathered onto her cheek. She stood up and squeezed past the Australians to push her face up to the small stream of air at the window in the corridor. I tried to fold my map of Bosnia into a fan, but moving my arm was too much effort.

The evening cooled, the other passengers stood up

and stretched, as if waking from hibernation. Most were backpackers, wearing flip-flops and crumpled shorts, and carrying rolled up sleeping bags. The girl opened her eyes and reached for her water bottle. I eyed it enviously. James and I had run out so we were drinking the warm vodka and multifruit juice we'd bought at the station. I flicked through the photocopies of my guidebook. *Sarajevo is beginning to attract visitors for more than its warring past...* I skimmed the pages then looked up to see the girl turning a wedding ring on her finger. She examined her hand, then eased the ring off and placed it in a small velvet string bag. She caught my eye and I said, 'I can't believe the heat. I thought we were going to be cooked alive.'

'The train is always like this,' she said. 'Boiling in summer, freezing in winter.'

I couldn't figure out her accent. 'Where are you from?'

'Sarajevo. I live in Toronto, but I flew to Budapest.'

She told me she was studying engineering in Toronto. She was coming back to visit her mother. I said I was from Manchester, while James watched us through half-open eyes. I told her I was interviewing people I met round Europe for a kind of writing project and I'd like to chat to her about Bosnia.

James sighed and folded his arms.

'Sure. Why not? I'm Aida.'

'I'm Yvonne,' I said.

James and I booked into a hostel on 'Pigeon Square', which packed budget travellers into 12 and 15-bed dorms. We were prepared with our earplugs and mosquito spray. In the morning we looked out at the *srbilj* ('*Built in 1891,*' I read aloud), at the low-roofed cafés and polished cobblestones, then at our photocopied guide. We decided to go on the hostel's 'War Tour' because it didn't involve walking. We were driven in a minibus out of the Baščaršija quarter *where behind the tourist panache Sarajevo keeps its soul* ('Will you stop reading it aloud,' said James); over the Princip Bridge *where the assassination of Arch Duke Ferdinand ignited WW1* (I muttered) past houses covered in potholes and shell marks and buildings patterned with bullets, and then up steep roads to the remnants of the bobsleigh runs from the 1984 Winter Olympics.

We walked along one of the tubular tracks. It was battered and broken, like a relic from a lost age. It curved up into the trees to a jagged end amidst the branches. James and I joined two lads for photos. We sat in a row on the track, pretending to be bobsleigh drivers and giggling. James was wary of the two lads till we found out they were married to each other.

Our guide was a young boy. In his long shorts and trainers he didn't look old enough to remember the war. He sipped from a can of Coke and told us how the Serbs shot at the Bosnians from these vantage points and pointed to houses only yards from the tree-lined cliff. We looked over the edge and at each other, as if expecting something more. As we piled back into the minibus to go to the tunnel I thought about the girl on the train. I'd text her. I was curious to find out her story.

We drove to the outskirts on the west of Sarajevo where the buildings hadn't been renovated. The houses were cracked with shell marks. 'This way,' the boy guide said. We were at a small house. 'This is the Tunnel Museum. It was built in 1993.' We followed him into a back garden, where there was a tunnel dug into the ground. The garden was lush, full of blackberry bushes and pear trees. Behind it were fields.

'The tunnel was 800 metres long and was used to smuggle food and supplies during the siege,' the boy guide was saying. The interior of the house had been turned into a museum. We peered at the empty shell cases, bullets and camouflage equipment. The boy guide handed round an old shell. We felt its weight in our hands, its rusty smoothness.

'Look at it!' I said to James. He shrugged and took it. Then a rifle was passed around and a man pretended to fire it. The guide told us about war tactics, ammunition and how the Serbs had surrounded the city, pointing to places on a map.

'What is this?' James whispered. 'War Disneyland?'

Later, James and I climbed down wooden steps into the hole in the garden, and crouched in the tunnel. I felt the wooden boards under my sandals and stroked the corrugated iron walls. I tried to imagine struggling through the water, carrying supplies. A few feet down it was blocked off with bricks. Outside, I looked at photos of men climbing out of the tunnel. A man in a football cap confided to a woman, 'This tour's a joke. There's nothing to see.'

'Have you done Auschwitz?' she asked.

'Yeah. That was heavy. And Birkenau.'

James rolled his eyes at me. '"Have you done Auschwitz?"' he whispered. 'It makes me sick.' We wandered into the garden and I told James about the time I went to see the flattened remains of the concentration camp in Krakow. The one in *Schindler's List*. There was nothing left, just a field, some knocked over gravestones (it was built on a Jewish graveyard) and next to it, an abandoned house the guidebook said was used for interrogation by a member of the SS. Two lads I'd met and I had tiptoed in the open door and down to the cellar. We used our mobiles, one to light the way and the other to film the dark, empty rooms till we scared ourselves silly. It was weird, like the *Blair Witch Project*.

James looked at me. 'You filmed it?'

James and I spent the afternoon wandering round the Turkish quarter, looking at the bazaars, the bronze coffee pots and tiny cups. I texted Aida, and she agreed to meet at seven in Café Atriksa. James and I stopped for a coffee and sat on plush chairs outside a café. We dropped large sugars into our tiny coffee cups and nibbled Turkish delight. I tried to tell James more about my project. I wasn't sure about its shape yet, or whether it would be journalism or creative non-fiction, but its inspiration was Trotsky's words: 'You may not be interested in war, but war is interested in you.'

'Can't we just enjoy our holiday?'

I sat back on the cushion. 'I'm only telling you about it.'

'I don't go on about my PhD all the time, do I?'

'Sorry.'

His face was red. 'I mean,' he continued. 'You don't know what you're talking about. You don't know the first thing about war. Trotsky didn't even say that. He was talking about dialectical reasoning.'

I could feel my eyes pricking.

'Don't. Don't cry at me.'

I got up and went to the toilet to splash my face. It was a tiny cubicle. My nose was burnt and my eyes were red. I went outside and said, 'I'm going to meet the girl from the train. I'll see you later.'

I was still upset when I got to the bar, muttering 'dialectical fucking reasoning' to myself. The walls were covered in posters of The Stone Roses and Oasis. Aida was sitting in a chair at the back and clutching a small glass. Her hair was spiked and her jeans were ripped and patched. 'Hi,' she said. 'Do you want a šljivovica?'

'Yes please.'

We chatted about Sarajevo and the tour I'd been on, while the brandy made my face feel hot. 'I can't believe they have turned it into a tour,' she said. She had never seen the tunnel, though her father had gone through it for supplies. She told me she'd had an awful day avoiding her mother's questions about who she lived with in Toronto. Her mother was glad it was not with a man. Aida said she was engaged to a woman who was a Serbian immigrant. Of course her mother knew something was up, and kept prying, but she was ailing and Aida didn't want to cause her anymore stress, so she kept lying and saying she was single. I told her about the two married lads. 'Are you engaged to James?' she asked.

'God no. But we argue like a married couple.'

'So what do you want to know?'

'Just wanted to ask you about the war.'

'That's the first thing they ask me in Toronto. *So were you in the war?* I usually say I wasn't.'

I sipped some more of my drink. 'You're supposed to drink it like a shot,' she said. She drank hers in one go and said, 'Anyway, a lot of it is a blur. I was only ten when it started.'

Aida remembered standing on a chair, flicking the light switch on and off. 'It doesn't work,' she said.

Her father was sitting at the kitchen table. 'Everything is falling apart,' he said. Her mother was moving bedding into the kitchen. 'Don't bother your father,' she said. 'Hold these.' She passed Aida some pillow cases.

'Are we sleeping in here?' Aida asked.

'Yes. You're not to go in the bedrooms.'

'Why?'

'Will you try Zudha again?'

He sighed and dialled her number.

'Can I speak to her?' Aida asked.

'How are things there?' He asked, placing his hand flat on the table. 'Your mother wants you to come home.' He patted the wood, saying, 'I know, but we'd feel better if you were here.'

Then he looked at the phone and jabbed at the button. 'It's gone dead.'

Aida sat on her put-up bed with her drawing book. She was trying to focus on her picture, but she couldn't with the noise outside. She hated the sounds: the low rumble, the crackle of fires, and she hated sleeping in the kitchen.

'Can't you do something useful?' Her mother was trying to drag the kitchen table from the centre to the wall. 'Get up,' she said to Aida's father. 'I need to sort this room.'

He turned over on the other put-up bed. It creaked and sagged in the middle. 'I was dreaming,' he said. 'The library was burning. I was trying to save the books. I was holding onto them and falling.'

'It's always the books. The precious books. What about people?'

'You don't need to rearrange the kitchen again.'

Aida's mother heaved the table over and pushed the chairs under it. 'Why can't you do something instead of lying there? Why can't you go to the tunnel? ' She looked around the kitchen. 'Aida. We need to move your bed.'

Aida's coloured pencils were stubs. She was sitting at the table and drawing in brown, orange and grey – her least favourite colours. Red, yellow and pink were saved in her pencil case. She was drawing what she'd like her father to get from the tunnel. Chocolate, baklava and new pencils. There must be a shop at the other end of the tunnel, beyond the airport. It was run by nice old women wearing scarves.

'Bedtime,' her mother said.

Aida shook her head. She wanted to draw a bomb with a fizzing fuse. Boom. Aida and her parents flying through the air. She'd use her browns and greens to do it.

'Come on.'

There was a knock at the door. 'It's me!' Her father called. 'Look what I've got,' he said, leading in a goat.

'What?'

'It's for Aida,' he said. 'And we can have milk.' His face was streaked with dirt and his clothes were damp up to his chest, as if he had waded through a river. He dumped the bags on the table.

'Are you mad? Where are we going to keep it?'

'I'll put a nail in the wall and tie it there for now,' he said, but he slumped on a chair, holding onto the leash. Aida edged over, held out her hand and stroked the goat's head. It had tufts of brown fur around its ears, while its thin body was white with brown specks, though it was very dirty. She was pleased. 'Let's call her Nina.'

Her mother unpacked the bags. She placed flour, potatoes and cabbage on the table and then stared at them. Aida was looking forward to a meal without nettles. She was sick of nettles; they were worse than cabbage.

'I'm going to take some flour next door,' her father said.

'Why?'

'Old Petrovic asked me to get some flour. They paid for it.'

'Never mind them. They should have left already.'

Her father picked up a bag of flour and walked out. He used to play chess with Mr Petrovic. They'd play at a table on the pavement outside their apartments, and Aida would sit on the kerb.

'I don't think you should,' her mother called, but he had already gone.

*

'Where is your house? I asked Aida.

'I can show it to you. It's not far. North of Pigeon Square. 'Want to see it?'

'I'm supposed to be meeting James,' I said, looking at my phone. A message from James said: 'Are you still out?'

'He can wait,' I said, putting the phone in my pocket.

We left the bar. The road was crowded with tourists looking at the gift shops, which were still open on Ferhadija. We walked to Pigeon Square and I filled my bottle with water from the fountain. 'My hostel's just here,' I said. A group of backpackers were queuing outside.

We walked up the steep hill next to the hostel and turned left onto a street of apartment blocks, then right onto a road where most of the apartments were boarded up.

'This is it.'

'Which was yours?'

'That one.' She pointed to the end block. 'The ground floor apartment. The bedrooms at the front were destroyed.'

The house was potholed like the buildings we'd passed that morning. The walls were blackened and part of the roof had fallen in.

'And that's where our neighbours lived,' she said, pointing to a boarded up window.

*

In the early morning, Aida would peer out the corner of the kitchen window and see the mountain peaks and everything would look peaceful. Perhaps there weren't any snipers up there at all. Or perhaps they were having a lie-in. Then she'd look down and see the holes in the buildings and the piles of rubbish and her mother would call her away from the blackout paper.

'You can't lie here forever,' her mother said. 'Just get up. Do something!' she said. 'What's wrong with you?' Her voice got higher. 'Why can't you be a man?' She slapped him on the arm. 'Just do something.' But he turned away from her. She sat on the bed, and started to rock back and forth.

Aida was curled on the other bed. She crept over to Nina and wrapped her arms around the goat's neck, but Nina was scared and pulled on her rope, wriggling out of Aida's grasp.

'Come in Ferid. What do you want?' Her father said.

'How is Zudha?'

'She is with her *husband* in Foca,' Her father said. 'We haven't heard from her in months.'

Ferid nodded, leaning on the table. Aida remembered him. He had courted Zudha, but her father had never liked him. He used to wear a leather jacket and would screech up and down the road on a scooter. Just before the war, Zudha had met the neat-looking Murat, and married him instead. Now, Ferid looked different. The leather jacket was replaced by a long coat, which hung loosely from his shoulders. 'You need to leave your house tonight,' he said. 'This building won't be safe.'

'Why? Is this to do with old Petrovic?'

'Don't ask why. You can stay at Sonja's at number 26.'

When it was dark they left the apartment, crept along the side of the road, and into Sonja's apartment.

Sonja let them into her kitchen. There was a bed by the wall and a mattress on the floor. 'You can sleep here.'

'Thank you.' Her father brought in bags of clothes, the tin stove and the remains of food. He led in the goat and Sonja told him to tie it to the door.

Aida went to sleep between her parents. She woke and one side of her was cold. She blinked and when her eyes became used to the dark, she saw that her father was sitting at the window and stroking Nina. He eased back the blackout paper and peered through the glass. When Aida woke again, just as it was getting light, he was still sitting there, his head to the side and his mouth hanging open, snoring.

The next evening they returned home. Her father stopped outside their neighbour's house. Inside the window was black and charred. 'Come on,' her mother said, heading to their door. At the back of their house, their kitchen was the same as they had left it except the windows had shattered. Aida perched on the bed, shivering in her coat. Her mother tried to get the stove going while her father put cardboard up at the windows.

Later, Aida would look through their neighbour's window frame at the burnt out kitchen and imagine Mr Petrovic still in there. He would be sitting at the dining table, as if he was waiting for his dinner to arrive, with his knife and fork in his hands, and his wife would be cutting bread and chatting to him.

★

I found my cardigan in my bag and put it on. It was cold up here. You could see the mountains on the other side of the city. I started to text, but stopped.

What do you know? Stop going on about your writing.

I wanted to get my bag from the hostel and disappear into the night. I'd travel round Europe, researching on my own. But I knew in reality I'd slope back to the hostel and crawl into my bunk, with nothing to do but listen to his breathing below.

Aida was also checking her phone. She looked up at the burnt out buildings around us, the craters in the brickwork, and placed her phone back in her pocket.

'So what are you going to do with all these stories then?'

'I'm not sure yet.'

We walked down the road. Aida was silent, staring at the ruins around us.

'What happened to the goat?' I asked.

'We couldn't feed her and one day she ran away. We never found her.'

'Oh.' I hugged my arms around myself. 'And your sister?'

'I'm not talking about my sister.' Aida's voice was bitter, angry almost. I stopped, and wondered if I should get back to the hostel.

'Let's go up here,' she said, pointing up the steep road.

'At the top, there's a park with a cliff and a great view of the city.'

One side of the road was lined with houses and on the right there was a cemetery with white gravestones, lit up by lamps. I stared at the gravestones and then turned to look at the city. Dotted amidst the streets and houses there were other cemeteries, lit like this one. I searched in my bag for my camera, but paused. I could hear the sound of singing: a low and mournful voice coming from nearby.

'What's that?'

'The call to prayers,' Aida said, pointing to a loudspeaker tied to a lamppost. We sat on the cemetery wall and listened.

33 Bullets

THE CROWD PUSHES Devrim towards the doors. He coughs, the smoke burning his throat and mouth. Someone knocks the back of his knee – his bad knee – and his legs buckle, so he grabs the denim–clad shoulder in front of him as the corridor widens into a foyer. 'Stand back, stand back!' shouts a guard. The doors open and Devrim is propelled outside. More and more people spill out of the doors, so he limps towards the grass where others have collapsed, coughing. He sinks to the ground, squinting in the bright sunlight. Ahead, he can see four men running towards a fence. He reaches for his plastic bag of papers, but of course, he doesn't have them.

First Tier Tribunal
(Immigration and Asylum Chamber)

<u>THE IMMIGRATION ACTS</u>
Before
IMMIGRATION JUDGE BLAIR
Between
DEVRIM BADR
<u>Appellant</u>
and
THE SECRETARY OF STATE FOR THE
HOME DEPARTMENT
<u>Respondent</u>
Representation:

<u>For the Appellant:</u> Ms Waters of Counsel.

<u>For the Respondent:</u> Mr Barker, Presenting Officer.

DETERMINATION AND REASONS

The Appellant is a citizen of Iran born on 25 September 1957 and appeals under section 82 of the Nationality, Immigration and Asylum Act 2002 against the respondent's refusal of his asylum claim under the 1951 Geneva Convention Relating to the Status of Refugees and the 1967 New York Protocol (hereinafter referred to as the Refugee Convention).

In the alternative, the Appellant's claim is to be considered on the basis that he may be entitled to humanitarian protection under the Immigration Rules insofar as they bring into domestic effect Council Directive 2004/83/ EC on minimum standards for the qualification and status of third country nationals, or stateless persons as refugees, or as persons who otherwise might need international protection.

Further, the Appellant claims that his removal from the UK would amount to a breach of his rights under Articles 2, 3 and 8 of the European Convention for the Protection of Human Rights and Fundamental Freedoms (hereinafter referred to as the Human Rights Convention).

'Qu'écrivez-vous?' Japhet was lying on the other bed, his arm drawn over his eyes. 'Vous écrivez tout le temps.' He sat up, making a writing movement with his hand.

'Je suis...' Devrim said, faltering. 'A book... about poetry.'

'Êtes-vous un poète?'

'No, no.' Devrim shifted on his bed, picking up his notes and papers. Everybody assumed he was a poet. He had written verse, but he had only ever shown it to his wife, who had said, 'Very nice, Devrim,' the way she might praise a child.

'I am a professor of Kurdish literature,' he said, but Japhet had turned to face the wall, his blue t-shirt stretched over his spine, revealing a thin scar down his neck. When Japhet had undressed, Devrim had seen other scars on his protruding ribs and back. Perhaps he had been beaten or tortured. It was hard to tell because in the last five days Japhet had hardly spoken or moved from his bed; he was just lying there, waiting to be deported. Devrim had seen a lot of people like that in the removal centres; people slumped on beds and chairs, or shuffling around, shoulders so hunched they might topple over. At least he had his research to keep him going. He was in the middle of writing an article on the poetry of Ahmed Arif, and he made sure he wrote everyday while stretched on his bed. Not that there was anywhere to go, just the canteen for meals and an hour in the yard, where he would smoke his daily cigarette. On the first day he had offered Japhet one but he was only interested in the lighter, which had a tiny floating naked woman in it. A campaigner, who had visited Devrim in Harmondsworth, had given it to him, along with two pairs of Union Jack underpants.

He had already spent time in Colnbrook, and two other Immigration Removal Centres. They kept moving him around, for no reason he could fathom. This facility was smaller than the others and overcrowded. The cell was smaller too, with just enough room for the two beds, toilet and sink, as well as the stale smell of cooped up bodies.

He shifted the pillow under his knee. It was swollen again, but there was no point asking for a doctor in here.

The Appellant's Claim

The Appellant's claim may be briefly summarised as follows. He claims he worked for the University of Tehran as Professor of Persian and Kurdish literatures. On 25 June 2006 the Appellant was getting off a train at Shahid Madani station in Tehran, when armed police led him out of the station and forced him into a car. Here, they placed a hood on his head and drove him to an unknown prison. He claims he was kept in a cell for three months, where he was interrogated and tortured for information on Kurdish rebels and their whereabouts. He was accused of 'crimes against national security,' which included supporting Kurdish separatism and being an active member of the PKK. He was accused of spreading Kurdish propaganda to students through his research into Kurdish poetry and literary culture.

The Appellant claims he was released without explanation. He returned home to find his house had been raided and his wife's corpse in the kitchen. He claims she had been stabbed numerous times.

The Appellant seemingly fled Iran to Turkey and from there flew to the UK, using, by his own admission, a false passport.

Burden and Standard of Proof

I am reminded that the burden of proof is on the Appellant to establish that he comes within the definition of a refugee under the Refugee Convention as being a person outside his country who by reason of a well founded fear of persecution for reason of race, religion, nationality, membership of a particular social group or political opinion is unable, or unwilling, owing to such fear to avail himself of the protection of that country.

The standard of proof is whether there is a reasonable likelihood that the Appellant would face persecution for a Convention reason if returned to Iran and I have applied that standard when looking at the evidence before me.

Only if I am not satisfied to the required standard

that the Appellant is not a refugee can he then qualify for humanitarian protection. The burden then rests upon the Appellant to show there are substantial grounds for believing that if returned to Iran he would face a real risk of suffering serious harm and is equally unable or, owing to the risk, unwilling to avail himself of the protection of that country.

When considering the Appellant's claim under the Human Rights Convention the burden and standard of proof remain the same.

Devrim woke and reached for a piece of paper from the pile beside his bed. He sat upright, muttering: 'This is the Mengene mountain... When dawn creeps up to lake Van.' He found his pen from under his pillow. 'This is the Mengene mountain...' he repeated, scribbling the words down. 'Fugitive pigeons at water pools... something something... and partridge flocks.'

His memory wasn't what it was; he should have spent years memorising poetry instead of writing about it.

'Devrim!' Japhet moaned, pulling his cover over him.

'Sorry.'

He pulled his A4 pad from under his pillow. He'd written exactly two paragraphs of his article, 'Ahmed Arif and The Forms of Resistance in Kurdish Poetry.' Two paragraphs in five weeks. Back home he would have finished it in days.

Kurdish poetry has long been a means of fighting the hegemony of ruling cultures. Since the emergence of a Kurdish literature in the eighteenth and nineteenth centuries when poets began to write in the dialects of Sorani and Kurmanji instead of the ruling languages, Kurdish poetry has given breath to Kurdish resistance against persecution.

The poet Abdulla Goran revolutionised Kurdish poetry by writing in the patterns of Kurdish folk songs instead of traditional Arabic metres. For the recent generation of Kurdish poets, such as Farhad Shakely, Ahmed Arif and others, free verse, folk songs and the rhythms of Kurdish speech are all strategies in their poetry of resistance, even when being incorporated into the language of the oppressor, in Arif's case Turkish.

He frowned at the page. He couldn't work in this cell; he just couldn't concentrate. How he missed his books and desk in his university office, where it was cool in the mornings and he would write with coffee before the queue of students grew in the hall. He had been the nominal Kurdish lecturer; he doubted his colleagues had made much of a fuss about his disappearance; people disappeared and then they were forgotten.

He needed to contact a university. That's what Zeinab would suggest. She'd always known what to do. 'My academic *peshmerga*,' she'd called him. But it was Zeinab who was the *peshmerga*. Not him. She'd campaigned for women's rights, Kurdish rights, spent evenings printing leaflets and in meetings with other women.

Anyway, he'd always imagined freedom fighters wearing red turbans, riding horses and waving Kalashnikovs. They were romantic figures, with lined, leathery faces, and squinting eyes, and probably very different to the men hiding in the Qandil mountains. He had played *peshmergas* when he was a child, but he was usually cast as the evil militia, jumped on by his brother Bahma and the other boys, and then sat on till his mother shooed them away and recruited him as her thread holder. He'd liked holding the spools between his hands, as she wove, intent and frowning. And from all the thick coloured threads, a carpet emerged. That is the memory he returns to, his mother weaving and beyond her the mountains, grey-tipped and hazy in the heat.

When he moved to the city with Zeinab, he'd tried to

encourage her to weave carpets, but she'd had no inclination, even though he bought her threads and wool. 'You do it, then,' she'd said. 'You make your carpet. I have better things to do.' She still liked to call him, 'my academic *peshmerga*,' as if he was an intellectual revolutionary.

But he could still see the dried blood on the wall; the wide mark by the table, the upturned chairs, and the books scattered on the floor. No, he couldn't think of this.

The Respondent's Case

The detailed reasons for the Respondent's Decision is set out in the Home Office Reasons for Refusal letter dated 24 June 2007, and calls into question the credibility and plausibility of the Appellant's account.

The Appellant's Case

On behalf of the Appellant Ms Waters relied upon her detailed skeleton argument. She submitted that the Decision is not in accordance with the law and is against the weight of evidence; that the Appellant's claim is credible. And that he has established a well founded fear of state persecution for the Refugee Convention Ground of Race, i.e. ethnic persecution.

Devrim returned from the canteen with two slices of white bread stuffed in his pocket, wedged together with margarine. The food in here was disgusting; he'd seen people vomit after eating and one man had thrown his bowl against the wall and been dragged out by the guards. The place smelt, not as cooking should, all aromatic and spicy, but of rotten cabbage and frying oil. In the lunch queue, there had been talk of a charter flight. Some said Cairo. Others Nairobi. Sometimes you were warned about your deportation. Often, they just dragged you from your cell.

While he had been listening to the talk in the queue he

realised that Japhet must be going on the next charter flight. That was why he was so depressed.

Japhet was lying on his back, his bare feet dangling off the edge of the bed. 'Here you are,' Devrim said. 'Some bread. Sorry, it is...' He pulled out the squashed bread, and placed it next to Japhet's shoulder.

Japhet turned on his side and picked up the bread, squeezing it between his fingers. He sniffed it, then he seemed to lose interest, and dropped it on the floor. He lay on his back again, with his arm over his eyes.

In the night Devrim had heard Japhet counting in French, and in another language he didn't recognise. Over and over he'd count. *Un, deux, troi, quatre, cinq...* like a kind of mantra, or prayer. No, a poem. The numbers were a poem. Devrim found his pen and wrote: *Poems are necessary to survival. We all make them out of the words we have.*

It was early afternoon. He wouldn't bother with his daily cigarette in the yard. He'd try to get some work done instead. On the PC available for the detainees' use, he had checked the *The International Journal of Kurdish Studies*. The deadline for the next issue was Tuesday. Two days and he had still only written a couple of pages.

Ahmed Arif's poem is evidence of the political power of poetry both on and off the page. '33 Bullets' is an eulogy for thirty-three Kurds who were machine gunned in 1943 for having connections with Kurds on the other side of the border; their village had been divided by the Versailles Treaty in 1923, and they were, as the poem said, not used to passports. One man survived the massacre and managed to cross the border to his relatives. The poem was later recited by imprisoned Kurds and its enunciation became a form of resistance.

Devrim looked up from his article to find a man kneeling beside Japhet's bed. The man, who was tall and thin like Japhet, murmured into his ear. He nodded and pulled himself up.

My Findings of Credibility and Fact

In determining this appeal, there are many aspects of the Appellant's account that I find are inherently implausible and overall there is a series of disjointed claimed events with no given rational and causal explanation.

I find that there is no reason given for the arrest and detention or of his release.

The Appellant seems to have forgotten material aspects of what he was interrogated about and accused of. He is not able to corroborate his story with any evidence. There is no proof of his incarceration or alleged torture.

By 8pm Devrim's stomach was rumbling. He had missed the evening meal to keep working. Perhaps he could eat the slices of bread off the floor. Japhet wasn't lying down now; he was perched on the end of his bed, his arms folded, staring at the wall. Devrim pushed his papers aside, and reached over to grab the bread. 'Would you like this?'

'Non, non.' Japhet shook his head.

Devrim stuffed the bread into his mouth, but then stopped chewing. A woman had begun to wail; a long, mournful cry coming from a cell down the corridor. He chewed slowly as another woman joined in. The notes of the wailing grew higher, and wavered up and down, almost as if in harmony.

The cells weren't locked yet, so he got up to peer round the door. Two guards rushed past and barged into an adjacent room. Japhet gestured to let him see, so Devrim stepped aside and tried to look over Japhet's shoulder, but it was hard as he was so much taller.

Another guard was passing and closed their door.

Devrim heard it lock, and the other cells locking too, but this didn't block the sound of wailing.

Japhet leaned against the door, his arms folded. Devrim sat on his bed, muttering:

Shoot, bastards
Shoot me
I do not die easily
I am live under the ashes
I have words buried in my belly

Dear guardian, write my story as it is
Otherwise, they might call it a rumor
These are not rosy bosoms
But a dumdum bullet of a barrel
Broken in my mouth

Japhet sat next to Devrim so he began reciting the poem again, and for once he could remember almost every word. When he had finished he turned to look at the other man.

'Pourquoi?' Japhet said, scattering the papers across the bed. 'Quel est le but?'

Devrim gathered his papers together, patting them and neatening them on his knee.

'It's important,' he said.

Japhet stared at him.

No one understood that if his work was accepted by a journal, he might get a book contract, and when he was recognised as an authority on Kurdish literature he might get special dispensation to stay in the UK. 'With this,' he said, holding up his work, 'they won't deport me!'

Japhet frowned. 'Deport,' he said. 'They deport you... me... ' He gestured around the room. 'Tout le monde. Est-ce que vous comprenez?'

I do not believe that the Appellant is under threat in his home country. He claims both to be a supporter and to be neutral concerning matters of Kurdish independence. If he is neutral then he has nothing to fear from the government. If he is a supporter of PJAK then he could be said to support a known violent terrorist group [and therefore fears only legitimate prosecution].

Likewise, I doubt his legitimacy as a professor of literature. There is no Devrim Badr. He claims to have published articles in various online journals under the pseudonym Abbas Herii, but there is no evidence of this provided.

I conclude from the forgoing that the Appellant is simply not an honest and truthful witness. I have no doubt that the account is an elaborate and deliberately disjointed fabrication in order to gain access to the UK.

The Appellant claims that he fears persecution by the state. In the light of the facts which I have found, I have come to the inevitable conclusion that the Appellant has failed to show that such fear is well founded. I am not satisfied that he was subjected to persecution whilst in Iran, and on the evidence available to me, I am not satisfied that he would be subject to persecution on his return.

In the morning, Devrim got up to open the cell door, but it was still locked. He rattled it and went back to his bed. It was Monday and he wasn't going to be able to finish his article in time. He tidied his pile of papers and lay back on the pillow. Japhet was sitting with his back to the wall, strumming his fingers on his knee.

Devim had seen all this before; they were locked up so it was easier to collect them for the charter flight. He fluffed up his pillow and settled himself against it, murmuring the words of Ahmed Arif over and over.

By the afternoon, Devrim was starving. He could hear the guards patrolling, but the wailing had died down. He sat up at the shouting in the corridor and the sound of running feet.

Japhet put his ear against the door. He turned round, his eyes bright, saying, 'Donnez–moi le briquette,' and making a lighter motion with his hand.

Devrim rummaged through his things for his lighter and gave it to him. 'What are you doing?'

Japhet knelt down and held the lighter against the corner of his bed sheet. The material caught light, but then went out. He muttered something, and tried again.

'You need paper,' Devrim said. He stared at his work, at the lines of writing, the scribbled, half remembered words of Ahmed Arif, the article he would never finish. He picked up the sheets of paper and the A4 pad and gave them to Japhet. 'This will help it burn.'

Japhet rolled up the pieces of paper, twisted them and made a pile amidst the bedclothes. Then he held the lighter to the edges of the paper till they crinkled and burnt, pushing the blanket into the flames.

'And these,' Devim said, reaching for the documents, the letters from the solicitor, the appeal proceedings. 'Burn these. All of them.'

Japhet added them to the growing fire. The flames licked around the paper and caught the sheets. There they went. All the papers. The last of his work. All gone. They looked at each other and laughed. The smoke rose in the air and an alarm began to shrill. They backed out of the way and crouched near to the door as the flames caught the sheets and the whole bed began to burn. Japhet pushed the other bed over so it caught fire too.

By the time the door opened, they were coughing and choking and the guards had to drag them out as smoke filled the corridor from fires in different cells.

*

Devrim is sitting on the grass with a group of women and children, while two little boys chase each other in a circle, as if following a line drawn on the ground. There are plumes of smoke coming from the north side of the detention centre. In the distance, holidaymakers trundle suitcases out of terminal doors, heading towards the roads and roundabouts.

He wipes his streaming eyes with the back of his hand, and drags himself up. Ahead, he can see that one of the sprinters is Japhet, and that he and the others have nearly reached the fence. Beyond it are fields and then the outline of a city.

He has nothing now. No papers, no article, no documents. Nothing. He can see the fence and he knows he can make it.

The Spartacist League

August 2, 1918: Breslau Prison

THE MORNING LIGHT hasn't yet reached Rosa's window, but she has been awake for hours. Somewhere in the prison, guards chatter, doors clang open; the rattle of keys and footsteps, then the humming of the cleaner. The overhead light flickers on, so Rosa eases herself off the bed and onto the bucket. She squats and steadies herself. There is nothing to use as toilet paper other than a portion of cloth, which she folds over and over. Then she washes her hands in the bowl of water. If only she were back in Wronke, where her room had a view of the garden, and it wasn't like a prison at all.

Rosa sits at her desk by the slit of a window. 'You take too tragic a view of my circumstances,' she has written to Mathilde Jacob. 'We have to take everything as it comes and find beauty in everything.' What platitudes. She opens her letter case, scrunches up the paper and starts again.

> Dear Mathilde,
> You are feeling embittered because of my long imprisonment. You ask: "How can human beings dare to decide the fate of their fellows?" You won't mind – I couldn't help laughing as I read. In Dostoevsky's novel, *The Brothers Karamazov,* one of the characters, Madam Hokhlakova, used to ask the same question. My dear little bird, the whole history of civilization

is grounded upon "human beings deciding the fate of their fellows"; the practice is deeply rooted in the material conditions of existence. Nothing but a further evolution, and a painful one, can change such things.

Usually she manages to convince herself with the optimism of her letters. But not today. 'Find beauty in everything.' She should write that on the wall. 'In everything.'

The bell rings its tinny, metallic sound as if it isn't a bell, but someone clanging a bucket. The guard – a kindly Polish woman – takes her to the paved courtyard for her exercise. The guard's skirts have been one of her main smuggling routes, but the only time she has taken any interest in Rosa's conversations on the imperialism of the war was when Rosa quoted Engels: 'The man is the bourgeois of the family, the woman represents the proletariat,' and the woman laughed and hugged her.

Her mother's favourite story was of Rosa teaching the servants to read when she was only five years old. She doesn't remember this; her first memory is of grey-coated doctors looming over her bed, spooning bitter liquid into her mouth. That was the year she was laid up with a misdiagnosis of TB of the hip and she was only carried downstairs on Sundays.

The pain in her hip is bad now. As she walks to and fro, she keeps her eyes on the grey paving stones and her mind away from the spasms up and down her left leg and deep into her thigh. She lets herself limp. At rallies she used to minimise her limp until she realised it helped people to trust her; they wouldn't listen to someone who walked like a lady.

With the toe of her boot, Rosa nudges a clump of grass spurting between the stones. See, hope is everywhere. But she can still see the prisoners at work on the other side of the yard, carrying wood and stones from one end to the other. The air is warm and bright, for it is August, but by the afternoon they will swelter and burn. Yes, she will write about the penal system. You can see how it is permeated with class oppression.

In 1914, her tracts had done little to stop them charging to the front to fight for their old masters; a war-mad populace. Class struggle and Social Democracy were nowhere more abandoned than they were in Germany. 'Workers of the world unite in peacetime,' she wrote. 'But in war slit one another's throats.'

She has spent most of the war in prison. Her secretary and friend, Mathilde, visits every month, bringing soap, bunches of flowers, and news from The Spartacist League, as the more prominent members - like Karl and Leo - have either been imprisoned or are in hiding. Sometimes Rosa places her head on Mathilde's lap, as if there is the only place she can breathe.

She takes another turn in the yard and stops to lift and stretch her left leg. Above her, the sun outlines the turrets and starlings flit in the sky.

'Rosa!' her guard calls from the doorway. 'There is someone to see you.'

In the visiting room, a woman is sitting on a wooden chair and holding her hat on her knee. She has dark hair, worn like Rosa's in a chignon at the back, though she is much younger, perhaps thirty years old. Her coat has been mended many times and her boots have worn thin. The woman stands, smiling, saying her name is Gertrude Schmidt, and she has come all the way from Berlin because she read *The Junius Pamphlet* and was inspired to find it had been penned by a woman; it spoke to her about the war and the wrongness of it.

Rosa perches on the other chair while Gertrude says that her husband had been a member of the German Social Democratic Party, but he had still gone to the front with the men at his ironworks, and died at the Somme.

'You don't know what it means,' Rosa says. 'For you to have come all this way to tell me this.' She moves her chair closer to Gertrude's. 'You have given me such hope.'

November 9, 1918

'Rosa!' Her guard rushes into the cell. 'You're to be released.'

'Why?' Rosa turns at her desk.

'An amnesty. All the politicals are going.'

'Amnesty? At night?'

The guard smiles, leaning against the doorframe. 'I'm sure they won't mind you staying another night.'

'Are there trains to Berlin?'

'Ha! We haven't had trains for weeks! But I will find out.'

In the morning, the trains are miraculously running again. Rosa packs what she can into two bags. There should be something more official about being set free, but her guard opens the door as if she has been staying in a hotel, and then catches Rosa in an embrace. As she walks down the road, Rosa waves goodbye.

The web of streets stretches out before her, and the autumn day is as cool and grey as slate. She takes the road that leads towards the centre of Breslau and the train station. On the bank of the Oder she pauses at the sound of a crowd chanting, and follows the noise back towards the town centre. Perhaps it is a rally or a march? So soon though? She comes out at the Marktplatz. In front of the town hall, people are gathered and listening to a man on a podium. Men with pinched, hungry faces push at the edges of the crowd.

She makes her way through till she gets to the podium. She tells the organisers that she is a member of the USDP and one of the leaders of the Spartacist League. She would like to address the crowd. They laugh and glance at each other. 'Help me up,' she says. So one shrugs and lifts her onto the podium.

She stands behind the lectern and the crowd grows quiet. 'My name is Rosa Luxemburg,' she announces.

'Get the Fräulein off!' someone shouts while others whistle and whoop.

'The imperialist war is over,' Rosa states, holding onto the lectern to steady herself. 'And Europe is drenched in the blood of millions. Shamed, dishonoured, wading in blood and dripping with filth, thus capitalist society stands.'

'Who is she?'

She pauses and looks out at the congregation. 'Not... as we usually see it, playing the roles of peace and righteousness, of order, of philosophy, of ethics – but as a roaring beast, as an orgy of anarchy, as a pestilential breath, devastating culture and humanity – so it appears in all its hideous nakedness.' She leans forward. 'The majority of those who have died have been our brothers, the working class.'

'Killers!' someone shouts from the right. 'Murderers!'

She looks at where the voice has come from. 'Yes,' she states. 'It is us who they sent to kill each other.'

'What do you know, sweetheart? You weren't sent!' This is from nearby, accompanied by laughter, but she continues to look out at the men before her.

'I have spent four years in prison because I spoke out against this war; I spoke out for you, so that you and your sons would not be trooped out as cannon fodder to die in the fields of France in a war that was not ours. It was not us we were fighting for, but for the beast of capitalism and its imperialist desires.'

The crowd has grown quiet. She speaks slowly now, turning to look at individuals at the front. 'The World War confronts society with the choice: either continuation of capitalism, new wars, and imminent decline into chaos and anarchy, or the abolition of capitalist exploitation. The means of production have been destroyed on a monstrous scale. Millions of able workers, the finest and strongest sons of the working class, slaughtered. Awaiting the survivors' return stands the leering misery of unemployment. Famine and disease threaten to sap the strength of the people at its root. The financial bankruptcy of the state, due to the monstrous burdens of war debt, is inevitable.

'But,' she says, holding her arm in the air. 'Already our brothers are rising up! The Navy has refused to fight; they have mutinied and it is spreading like a wildfire through Germany.' Her voice rises now till she thinks it might break. 'Now is the time, Brothers, to fan these flames because we can see that change is possible. Our comrades in Russia are leading the way. They have shown that this change can happen throughout the world. Stand together comrades. Make this change happen!'

A hand steadies her as her hip gives way and she stumbles on the stage. She coughs, grabbing hold of the lectern: 'This change will happen!'

Rosa climbs down and raises both hands as the crowd applauds and chants. The men beside the stage shake her hand and clap her on the back.

November 10, 1918

When Rosa's train arrives in Berlin Lehrter Bahnhof, Mathilde is standing on the platform. Around her, servicemen and families are waiting to board. Rosa struggles off the carriage with her bags. 'Mathilde!' she calls.

'Rosa!' Mathilde hurries over and hugs her. 'You... you look exhausted. Do you want to rest? You can stay at my rooms.'

'Of course not. Let's go to the offices.'

'We've occupied the *Berliner Lokal-Anzeiger*,' Mathilde says, taking one of Rosa's bags. 'Karl and everybody are there.'

As they cross the platform, Rosa notices a woman standing next to a news-stand, with a chignon and wearing a patched coat. 'Gertrude!'

Gertrude smiles, so Rosa walks over to her. 'Are you waiting for someone?'

'A friend from Munich but they weren't on the train...'

'This is Mathilde. Mathilde, this is Gertrude Schmidt who I wrote to you about.'

Mathilde shakes Gertrude's hand. 'Good afternoon,' she says.

'Come, Gertrude,' Rosa says. 'Come see the offices and you can meet everybody.'

At *The Berliner Lokal-Anzeiger*, Karl Liebknecht is talking to three men in the printing rooms. He too has aged from his imprisonment; his dark, curly hair is grey, and under his glasses, his eyes are lined and weary. 'Rosa, perhaps you can persuade these good comrades to continue printing,' he says. 'They seem to have had a change of heart.'

One of the men holds up his hands. 'I'm afraid these printers can no longer be used by the Spartacist League. We are determined to trust the government for peace and quiet and security of private property.'

'My dear comrade,' Rosa begins. 'Does your proletarian conscience not speak out against the atrocities?'

'No. I'm sorry. I have written to Ebert himself about this. I just cannot have it in my firm. You people will have to leave.'

'There are other printers, surely,' she whispers to Karl. 'This is proving nothing.' She turns to Gertrude, who is standing a little apart. 'Let's get something to eat, so you can meet everyone.'

They walk to Hotel Excelsior, where Wilhelm Pieck and Leo Jogiches are sitting at a large oval table in the dining area. At the door, Mathilde says she is going home. 'But why don't you stay for an hour or so?' Rosa says. 'It's been so long...'

Mathilde shakes her head and walks into the darkening street without saying goodbye.

At the table, Leo is ordering a round of beers with

bread, pickles and cheese. He doesn't see Rosa at first as she sits down next to Gertrude Schmidt. Rosa smoothes her hair, but she can't hide the grey or the creases around her mouth and eyes. Leo's face is more rugged and lined than she remembers, but his thick hair still stands up on his head; a thatch of coarse grey straw. He pauses, glances at her and then continues talking to the waiter.

Rosa fusses in her bag, trying not to look at him. The waiter returns with the round of beers and Leo stands up. 'A toast to Rosa's release!'

'Welcome back, Rosa!'

She smiles, holding up her beer.

'To the *Freie Sozialistische Republik!*'

Everybody clinks glasses again. The beer hits her empty stomach and her head spins.

Gertrude places her hand on Rosa's arm. 'I don't usually drink beer,' she whispers. 'What would my husband have said?'

Rosa smiles, nibbling some bread and cheese, thinking of the rally in Breslau and how the air of Berlin seemed restless; on the tram through Mitte they'd seen groups of young men talking on the roads, gusts of autumn leaves circling in the air; an aliveness. 'We are on the cusp of something,' Rosa says. 'Something great.'

'I want to be a part of it,' Gertrude says, leaning over. 'With my husband gone, I feel I have to do something. I have no children. I have nothing now.'

Rosa can smell the gherkins and beer on her breath. Around them the talk is loud and raucous; guests sitting at the other tables are peering at them. 'Now you have everything,' Rosa says. 'There is much to be done. We need to bring out a new newspaper. How are you as a stenographer?'

'I had a little training, but I've done nothing since I married.'

'That's fine. Why don't you help with the newspaper?'

'I'd like that,' Gertrude smiles, sipping more of her beer.

December 10, 1918

Rosa pauses in the kitchen of Karl's apartment to check she has everything in her bag: drafts, pen, comb, handkerchief, smelling salts – she'd felt faint yesterday. She has meetings all morning for their new weekly newspaper, *Die Rote Fahne*, and a visit to the soldiers' and workers' council in the afternoon. Then she will write till late with Gertrude.

She has been staying with Karl and his wife Sonja on Hallesche Straße for the past couple of weeks. Sonja has hardly changed from before the war; her hair is still thick and dark. Strands have fallen loose as she stands peeling potatoes over a bowl.

'Are you ready?' Karl asks, opening the front door.

'I don't know why you have to,' Sonja says. 'I just don't know *why*.'

'Sonja, you must understand...' Karl says.

'You are going to get yourselves killed. Both of you.'

'Please, Sonja, not today.'

Sonja drops the knife and marches into the bedroom.

'I'll go to her,' Rosa says.

'It's OK. She'll just work herself up again.'

'We should get going then,' she says, slipping on her gloves.

Outside, the pavement is icy, so she holds on to Karl's arm to stop from slipping. A tree lies on the road, its stump jagged in the air, and a building across the way seems to have been cracked open.

'Go ahead,' she says. 'I'll see you at the office. I can't go any faster.'

'No, no. We should turn here though. Look.' He nods towards two Freikorps in their trench coats, standing on the opposite corner. 'Come on. Quick.'

At the office on Königgrätzer Straße, Leo, Ernst and Wilhelm are sitting around a long table for the editorial meeting. Leo is at one end and Wilhelm is at the other. Leo seems tired as he glances at Rosa, but she busies herself with her gloves and hat. She isn't going to let him think anything, not now, not after so long.

It is colder than outside with the wind streaming through the cracks. The dirt on the panes blocks the light and the sight of the bombed out apartments across the street. If only there were coffee, but she is certainly not making it. Karl joins the others at the table as Gertrude comes in the room with a large pot and cups. She hands them round, smiling. 'Sorry the coffee is weak. We only have a small amount.'

Rosa takes her cup to the far table. She doesn't know what she'd do without Gertrude, who stays up all night typing her articles. Sometimes she sleeps on the chair at Karl and Sonja's, and rises early with Rosa to carry on working.

People will do anything for you, Sonja has said. *You should be careful of your power.*

Mathilde comes in from outside, carrying a bundle of papers. 'Mathilde,' Rosa says.

But she walks past her and goes over to Leo. 'Here you are.'

'Thank you,' Leo says, smiling up at her. Mathilde sits next to him and they start going over something together.

Rosa arranges her work on the table so she can plan her article on the National Assembly. But she can't help looking over at them. How can Mathilde work so closely with him? She hardly speaks to Rosa anymore as if their years of friendship have never happened.

She sips her coffee and tries to focus on the draft. She knows what she must write, that the Councils will be like lambs cuddling up to lions. They don't see the National Assembly for what it is: an outmoded legacy of the French bourgeois revolution and its illusions of a 'united people'. It is a counter-revolutionary stronghold, which Chancellor Ebert and his gentlemen friends will use to banish and cripple the class struggle.

She writes a little more and then glances up. Now, Leo is talking to Wilhelm about tomorrow's edition. He rubs his temple with the side of his hand; an old, familiar gesture. All those nights they would stay up drinking coffee and arguing about the cause. But she wouldn't want to return to those days with him, whatever being with him had actually meant: how he'd disappear for weeks; the recriminations; her shouting all night, trying to goad something, some feeling at least, out of him.

All that happened after her first stay in Warsaw prison. She'd just finished *Organisational Questions of Russian Social Democracy*, and was keen to raise a debate about a general strike. She'd had the energy to work fifteen hours a day, and he'd had enough energy to see more than one woman. When she complained, he said facetiously, 'But Rosa, you're married.'

One night she screamed out the window as he stormed down the street, hat in hand, 'Why won't you give me a baby? At least give me a baby!' A neighbour called from the apartment below, and in the morning, the landlady told her to move out.

Wilhelm lights a cigarette for Leo. She has always hated his smoking; the smell makes her sick, and he insisted on smoking in her bedroom.

She smoothes her hair back. There have been other lovers, but no one like him. He catches her eye and grins. She gives him a small smile; yes, there is only ever him.

December 24, 1918

There are no thoughts for Christmas; Rosa and the other members of the Spartacist League are marching with the strikers through the Tiergarten, where the linden trees are stark against the grey sky. The crowd is made up of veterans, some armed and wearing their worn out uniforms. 'Down! Down! Down!' they chant. As they approach Brandenburger Tor, she notices the Freikorps crouched next to the stone carriage and horses, poised with machine guns. Rosa can't see how far back the march goes, but there must be hundreds, maybe thousands of people shouting, 'Down! Down! Down!' as if the entire population is gathering here to say they have had enough. A veteran pushes into Gertrude so Rosa grasps her arm. On her left, Leo has his fist in the air as he chants, 'Down! Down! Down!' Rosa brushes against him, the rough tweed of his coat grazing her cheek.

'Down, down, down, down, down!' the protesters chant. 'Down, down!' A rifle butt bounces against Rosa's forehead.

'Sorry!'

'Are you OK?' Leo asks.

'I'm fine,' she says, rubbing her forehead.

'Let me see.' He feels her forehead. 'You'll get a lump.' He pulls her to him, and she inhales his familiar smell of tobacco and musty tweed. 'All our lives, Rosa,' he says, bending down to speak into her ear. 'This is what we have been working towards.'

'Yes,' she says. 'I feel we are...' and she pauses while he continues chanting; she can't say what she feels. She looks up at the curve of his cheek; the grey bristle; the brown of his eyes. After all these years and all their work together she has never truly known him: just the cause and the smoking and never being together properly; no marriage, no children, nothing. For Leo there could never be domestic happiness when there was the cause. 'Life is more than politics,' she'd said to him the night he strode down the road. 'The only point of politics is to increase happiness; without it we are nothing, just dry, dry dust.'

Another man knocks into Gertrude Schmidt. Rosa pulls herself away from Leo and grasps Gertrude's arm. 'Are you alright?'

'So many people! I've never seen so many people... it's frightening.'

'Stand between us,' Leo says, drawing Gertrude over. 'You'll feel safer here.'

January 1, 1919

'It's now or never,' shouts Karl across the table.

'We need to lead them,' comes from somewhere.

'No, no, no, we are not the leaders. That is not our role,' says Leo. 'They have to lead themselves.' He sits down again as Rosa finds a seat. Next to her are Wilhelm, then Franz Mehring and Ernst Meyer – all there for a meeting to inaugurate The Communist Party of Germany.

'We can't miss this moment. It's now or never,' Karl says, standing up.

'When I returned to Berlin,' Rosa says over the noise. 'When,' she repeats as the room quietens, 'I returned, I thought they were ready. At the protests, the rallies, they seemed ready, but I fear they aren't. We need to build on the workers' and soldiers' councils. We need to arm them with knowledge for what is in store. There needs to be more organisation, more education; they need to be prepared for revolution and what lies afterwards.'

'This can only happen through revolution!' Karl shouts over her.

'They need to be ready to lead themselves.'

'If we miss this opportunity, that will be it for another generation. Ebert will claim power, and all will be lost.'

She rubs the bridge of her nose, as if she can force the pain away. Someone taps her elbow. It is Gertrude with a glass of water. 'Thank you,' Rosa whispers. Gertrude smiles and goes back to her seat. The room erupts into shouting, so Rosa sips the water and closes her eyes.

They fall silent. She looks up. A man is leaning against

the door frame, his hands and shirt covered in blood. Behind him, another man slumps to the floor.

Leo leaps forward. 'Gertrude, are there any towels here?'

Gertrude looks about her, then rushes into the other room. Rosa follows and finds her sitting on a chair, with towels on her lap.

'What are you doing?' Rosa asks.

'Sorry. I'm just not very good with...' She holds the towels out, her hands shaking. 'Here.'

Rosa frowns and takes them through to Karl, who is kneeling next to the man on the floor. He packs them tightly round the man's chest, while everybody watches. The man's face is white, drained, and around him blood soaks onto the floorboards.

January 5, 1919

'Rosa? Are you there?' Karl knocks at her door.

'Come in,' she says, looking up from her work. It is early morning and she has just sat down at the desk in her new lodgings on Behrenstraße to write after a few hours of fitful sleep. It is difficult being in a new bed every couple of nights, but they have to keep on the move, especially now they are being vilified in the right-wing press.

'They're protesting at the Chief of Police's dismissal.' Karl sits on the other chair. 'The workers! They've taken over newspaper offices on Kochstraße - all because of Eichhorn.'

'We need to go over there,' Rosa says. 'I can't believe it. After he stopped Noske from sending in troops to dispel them.'

'Maybe they are ready. Are you OK walking?'

'Of course.'

They arrive at the council a little after midday. As they turn onto Kochstraße they see that barricades of sandbags and furniture are being erected at the ends of the road. They edge past the bundles of newspaper; the man on guard nods to them, pointing up the stairs.

Inside the building, men are crammed between desks and chairs. One is saying, 'We are a Revolution Committee. Committee not Group.'

'We should be a Revolutionary Command.'

Rosa and Karl edge into the room. 'As the leader of the Communist Party and the Spartacist League, I would like to offer you our full support,' Karl announces.

The room erupts into cheers and feet stomping.

'We are here,' says Rosa. 'To show our support and say that this precepts a new day, a new dawn in German society, in which we will overthrow the Ebert government.'

'I don't know,' a man says. 'We need to make Ebert listen to our demands. We need discussion.'

'Ebert is open to negotiations.'

The committee debates their next move and report that a number of ex-soldiers are bringing arms, and that workers are spilling into the area in their thousands.

She smoothes her skirt and stands up, resting her hands on the chair's back. 'Comrades. The men you talk about negotiating with - Ebert and Noske the Minister of Defence - they supported the war and the slaughter of millions. They have capitulated. You can't trust them.'

'Here, here!' someone shouts.

'Who let these intellectuals in?'

'This is ridiculous,' Rosa says to Karl. 'I'm having nothing to do with this if they succumb to negotiations with Ebert.'

Outside, it is beginning to rain and grey clouds swathe the sky, so Rosa buttons up her coat for the walk back to the office. She links arms with Karl, her face bent against the wind. Groups of young men congregate on street corners, but for once, they don't stop to talk to them.

January 8, 1919

Rosa creeps along the side of the road littered with debris and paper. In the twilight she can make out the barricade, and men – her comrades – crouching behind it, their rifles propped on bundles of newspapers. After writing all day, she'd needed to get out of the office and she'd left without telling anyone. She edges over the road to join the men and sits on the ground next to one wearing a tailored brown suit. They are just ordinary workers. Not even veterans, just two young men in office clothes and an older man wearing overalls, who every couple of minutes shoots at what appears to be an empty rooftop.

'What are you doing?' The man in the brown suit whispers to her.

'My name is Rosa Luxemburg. I am...'

'You should get inside!' He leans over. 'Get away from here, Fräulein.'

'Rosa!' Mathilde beckons from a doorway. 'Come away!'

She struggles up and hurries over to Mathilde. 'This way,' Mathilde calls. 'What are you doing? Come through here.'

There is a hail of gunfire and an explosion; heat spreads over her back. When Rosa turns she sees that the older man has been flung onto the road, and the two younger ones are slumped on the bails. The man who had spoken to her slides slowly back onto the ground; his face turns towards her; he has been hit in the jaw; the red tissue of his mouth, and blood, so much blood, but his eyes are open and he seems to be looking right at her, imploring her.

She realises she is screaming and that Mathilde is pulling her down the passage. They feel their way in the dark to its end, Rosa's hands on the damp walls, stumbling in the black, and then on through another alley and another. She can still hear the gunfire, but all she can see is the man in the brown suit, his eyes asking, *What can you do about this?* All the men lying dead around Europe, filling up the rotting sewer of history. *How can you change things Rosa Luxemburg?*

Somewhere in the alley she trips; she is heaving, crying and Mathilde is crying too. She leans against a wall, wrapping her arms around herself and taking ragged, deep breaths.

In Mathilde's apartment, Rosa collapses onto a chair while Mathilde puts a kettle on the fire. Kneeling at the grate, she says, 'I saw you heading towards the fighting and followed. What were you doing out there?'

Rosa presses her cold hands together. Yes, she was foolish to go into the street like that. 'I had to see what was happening,' she says.

The paper and wood begin to catch light. Mathilde goes to sit on the other chair. 'Those poor men.'

'Yes... they...' Rosa starts to shake, as if she might cry again, but then she pulls herself up, saying more firmly. 'Of course, it's because Noske and Ebert have given the Freikorps carte blanche. They are killing with impunity.'

'We sit here, writing and talking about revolution while men die in the street.' Mathilde gets up to pour the boiling kettle into a pot, and then hands a cup to Rosa.

'It's because men die in the street that we sit here talking about revolution.' She sips her tea, the hot liquid scalding her tongue, but it sends warmth through her. 'This tea is wonderful, thank you.'

'You should sleep here tonight. Where are you staying?'

'I have an attic room on Friedrichstraße, but we're moving to Frau Markaussohn's next week.'

'Her poor hands.'

'Yes. She was so brave about it.' Rosa watches Mathilde stirring her tea. She looks exhausted; her dark hair pulled back so severely, her eyes puffy; she too has aged like the rest of them. All these years as secretary and confidant, bringing everything Rosa needed when she was in prison. She puts her cup down and says, 'You have been distant lately.'

Mathilde stands up and stokes the fire. 'Sometimes Rosa,' she says. 'You can be careless of people.'

Rosa hesitates. 'You don't think that, do you... not really?'

Mathilde doesn't turn round, so Rosa says, 'It's a lonely life I've chosen, that *we* have chosen. We work every hour of the day. No family. No roots. No children. So when companionship and friendship comes your way you have to snatch at it.'

Mathilde gets up from the fire and pours her some more tea.

'My friendship with Gertrude Schmidt is nothing like what we have.'

'And you don't really know her,' Mathilde says, sitting down. 'She isn't even a good stenographer.'

'I can speak to you like no one else. Come back. Come work with me again.'

Mathilde leans over to grasp Rosa's hand. 'Of course I will.'

January 14, 1919

It is nearly 2a.m. and Rosa is working in the attic room on Friedrichstraße. She is sitting at a large desk with an oil lamp burning beside her. She picks at a plate of cheese and rye bread, which Mathilde brought a few hours ago. She will ironically call the article: 'Order Prevails in Berlin'. The tone must be defiant and angry about the Ebert government's so called victory when even now she can hear gunfire in the street.

She stares at the lamp's flame, seeing the worker

slumped on the office floor; the man in the brown suit looking at her as blood poured from his jaw. And now the mediators at *Vorwärts*. She writes:

> The government's rampaging troops massacred the mediators who had tried to negotiate the surrender of the *Vorwärts* building, using their rifle butts to beat them beyond recognition. Prisoners were lined up against the wall and butchered so violently that skull and brain tissue covered the floors.

Gunfire cracks and spits outside. She goes to the blacked out windows to peer through a gap in the paper. In the distance, a building is burning and there are sporadic flashes of light. She shivers and sits back down.

She will explain what has happened. The leaders of the revolution were half-hearted and vacillated, which was obvious when they couldn't decide what to call themselves. Even though the masses of Berlin were laying down their lives, the leaders were unable to take decisive action.

She breaks off a piece of hardening bread and nibbles it. This loaf was the last dear Mathilde had, but it is heavy and sticks in her throat. Of course, she shouldn't be surprised by the brutality of the government's troops. She dips her pen:

> Civil war is the name the bourgeoisie give to class struggle, and it would be insane to believe that capitalists would good humouredly renounce property, profit, the right to exploit. All ruling classes fought to the end, with tenacious energy to preserve their privileges. One has only to remember the Roman patricians and the medieval feudal barons, the English cavaliers and the American slave dealers, the Wallachian boyars and the Lyonnais silk manufacturers - they all shed streams of blood, they all marched over corpses, provoked disorder and criminality in order to clamp down and

defend their privileges and power.

But, as the oil lamp fades and she thinks she must get to bed, she can still see the man's gaping, bloody jaw as Mathilde pulled her away.

January 15, 1919

'They thought I was you,' Gertrude says, gripping Rosa's hand. 'You!'

It is early morning and they are in a deserted warehouse, silent apart from the rustle and squeak of mice. Rosa sits down next to Gertrude on a crate, while Karl and Leo stand over them.

'So what happened?' Leo asks.

'They came to the office and they thought I was Rosa. I was the last one there after the meeting. I was cleaning up before I went home.'

She tells them that the Freikorps were waiting outside the office; two of them wearing their trench coats and helmets. They arrested her, claiming she was Rosa, and took her to the headquarters in a hotel next to the Zoological Gardens. They dragged her inside and interrogated her.

Rosa clutches Gertrude's hand and strokes it. 'Did they hurt you?'

'No, not really. They realised pretty quickly that I wasn't you.'

'What did they ask?'

'Just where you all were. How to find you.'

'And what did you say?'

'I said I didn't know. I told them I was a cleaner – I *am* most of the time – and I hardly knew the people that worked there.'

'And they let you go?' Leo asks, kneeling next to her.

'Yes.' Gertrude wipes her face with a handkerchief.

'You have to be careful, Rosa. They're scouring the city.' She folds the handkerchief and places it on her knee. Taking a breath, she says, 'Are you at Frau Markussohn's?'

'Yes, but I think we need to move,' says Karl. 'We'll move tomorrow.'

Gertrude turns to Rosa. 'I haven't seen you. Where have you been?'

'Just working. That's all.'

'You're shivering,' Leo says, placing his coat around Gertrude's shoulders. She begins to cry into her handkerchief. 'I'll take her home,' Leo says.

By the evening, Rosa is too exhausted to get up from Frau Markussohn's bed. She dips a flannel in a bowl of water and places it on her forehead, but the cold makes her headache worse.

'Rosa, do you want some tea?' Frau Markussohn is at the bedroom door, bringing a smell of stew with her. 'I hope you have been resting. You can do your writing tomorrow.'

'Yes, thank you.'

'Here you are.' She awkwardly places the tea next to Rosa with her left hand. Some of it spills into the saucer. The fingers on her other hand are still bandaged.

'How are your fingers?' Rosa asks.

'Much better, thank you.'

Frau Markussohn has hardly spoken about her time in custody over Christmas, other than that they held her hand flat on a table and hit her fingers with a baton.

'I'll clean up in here tomorrow,' she says, leaving the room. Rosa sips her tea, thinking of Gertrude. *I told them I was a cleaner.*

Rosa begins to shiver. She wraps her arms around herself, and then suddenly with the realisation, nausea hits her, waves of it sweeping through her. Leaning over the side of the bed, she reaches for the chamber pot and heaves.

Gertrude's hands, so white and perfect. Untouched. That is why they let her go unscathed. She told them. She knew where they were staying and she told them!

Rosa slumps back on the bed, but after a few moments she makes herself stand up and go through to the kitchen.

'Rosa, you look ill,' Frau Markussohn says.

Rosa sits next to Karl at the table and rests her head on her hands.

'It's not that it was too soon,' Karl says, as if they are mid-conversation. 'It was Ebert's plan. The negotiations, the peace deal, it was all a hoax. He murdered the messengers and anyone he found. You knew he was going to do it. *You* warned them.'

Frau Markussohn places bowls of stew before them. 'Come on, eat, Rosa.'

'We should move again,' Rosa says quietly. 'I think we should move tonight.' She picks up her spoon, but puts it down again.

'Tomorrow,' Karl says. 'We'll move to Dahlem and lie low for a while; we'll regroup. Talks in factories. Build up the Communist Party.'

Karl is almost joyous as he makes his plans. The years they have worked together, side by side. Both imprisoned. The marches. The meetings. Hardly ever resting, with Sonja worrying about their health. Sonja. Sonja in her kitchen, asking *Why, why do you have to do this? Why? What is the purpose of it all?* Sonja is the one who will suffer the most. And Mathilde, dear, loyal Mathilde...

'Rosa, are you alright? Is it is your headache?' asks Frau Markussohn. 'You haven't touched your stew.'

'We should move,' she says again.

'It's delicious,' Karl says. 'Don't be so downhearted, Rosa. Things will seem better in the morning. We'll move then.'

Rosa says nothing; she can hardly find the energy to speak or lift her spoon.

'Oh. There's someone knocking,' Frau Markussohn

says. 'Shall I see who it is?'

'Yes,' says Karl. 'Remember the drill.'

All our lives this is what we've been working towards, Leo said in the Tiergarten as she inhaled his tweed and smoke. This morning, he placed his coat on Gertrude's shoulders and comforted her. Afterwards, will he be able to return to Warsaw without thinking of her? Will he be betrayed too?

From the hallway, Frau Markussohn says, 'No, I don't know anyone by that name. No. Yes, you can come in.'

She is followed in by three Freikorps in grey trench coats and round helmets that hide their eyes. One says, 'Are you Rosa Luxemburg and Karl Liebknecht?'

'No. No... I'm Bernhard Fritz and this is Ada Weber.'

'We have reason to believe that you are Rosa Luxemburg and Karl Liebknecht. We have your arrest warrant.'

As calmly as she can, she places her hands on the table, despite feeling her body tipping into a chasm, tumbling over and over into a thick blackness; the revolution has failed; that chance has passed; there is only her spinning, as if she is falling out of history into a deep unknown.

She could tumble into that darkness and never surface, but instead she sits back on the chair and lifts her head. The room is bright and the Freikorps as well as Karl and Frau Markussohn, are watching her. She thinks of Engels and his walks through Manchester. There was defeat in Manchester too. The Peterloo Massacre. The Chartist movement in Britain ended in defeat. So did the revolt of the silk weavers in Lyon in 1831, the uprising of the Parisian proletariat in 1848, and the Paris commune.

All our lives this is what we have been working towards.

She stands up, holding onto the edge of the table, and in this moment she is certain that defeat is only temporary; that this is part of the march to victory; that the revolution will rise up again, riding on white horses, and it will proclaim: *I was, I am, I shall be.*

She looks up at the three uniformed men. 'Yes, I am

Rosa Luxemburg,' she says, and knows in this single moment all that will follow: that the Freikorps will take them outside, push Karl and her into separate cars, and drive them to a hotel near to the zoological gardens, where one of them will inform the waiting officers that they have arrested the traitors who intended to overthrow the government and seize power for themselves.

In this moment, Rosa sees that Karl will be dragged into the foyer, his cheeks bruised and swollen, with her screaming his name behind him, and that an officer will hurl her outside where in front of a gathering crowd she will think they can't kill her, not in such a public place. She sees them knocking the side of her head with a rifle butt, and her falling to the ground, struggling to get up, and being hit again, the legs and boots around her spinning and blackening, and then being dragged into the back of a car, her face pushed into a man's lap.

And moments later, they will say, 'Do it now!'

She knows all this as she stands in Frau Markusson's kitchen, declaring that she is the woman they are looking for; she is Rosa Luxemburg. Just as she knows that eventually one of the Freikorps in the car will gently press his gun to her forehead, and she will look up at the rim of his helmet, beneath it seeing nothing.

The Breakfast She Had

IN THE DRY season Nadia would dream of rain, soft cooling rain, like freshly welled water that pours away sand from your roots, dust from your eyes.

She does not miss the sand. She would like to turn all the sand in Sudan to glasses. Like the ones she sees in shops. Tall, with glistening stems.

Amina squirms off Nadia's knee and balances between her legs, rocking with the bus. She likes to drink the rain. *Cup of rain*, she will say, with her mouth wide to the sky. *Cup of rain*. Amina is pretty in her uniform, her hair in neat, tiny braids that start at her hairline and reach to a top ponytail. She is watching a woman's handbag by her arm. She loves handbags. The woman clicks it open. Inside are treasures. Bursting purse. Lipsticks. Perfume. Cadbury's chocolate. Nadia wishes she had a handbag of treasures. Her bag is packed with complicated forms, leaflets and a purse of carefully counted money.

The woman is wafting herself with a newspaper. Across the aisle, Nadia notices a boy is shielding his nose. Blood stains his hands and cheek. She wants to offer him a tissue but turns to the window, which is dusty as if Manchester has had a sandstorm. She watches the passing shops, the café, the deli. Her scalp is hot and itchy under her khimar. She pulls the edge of the cloth away from her ear as the bus jerks to a halt. They are flung forward and she grabs the seat in front, holding onto Amina with one hand. The woman's handbag hits the floor, spilling purse and lipsticks. There are mutters

119

and shuffles from the passengers as they right themselves.

Bad driver! Amina says. *Bad driver!*

Ssshhh.

The bus lurches past the parked cars and stops. The driver steps out of his cabin, dazed, as if he has been in there a long time. He says something and jumps off the bus. Nadia wipes the window as he runs into a school car park. She holds up Amina to watch. They will be late for the register.

Her stomach clenches. She could not manage the Frosties this morning. What she wanted was the bowl of warm asida she used to have out by the neem trees with Amina asleep in her arms. Early, when the mists had cleared after a shower in the rainy season, the sun cooking the damp yellow earth and the sky over the heights of Jebel Marra, where she could see the coming sandstorms and downpours. After her husband Masood was up and dressed in a too-hot shirt, already damp under his arms as he walked to Nyala.

Masood was a picture: tall straight back, fat briefcase, tie too tight. But he was too proud to loosen it, proud to work in Nyala. She was also proud of his job in Mana Manufacturing. But he never said what kept him there late at night or what he discussed with his brothers while they ate and she waited in the kitchen. She barely dared to breathe in the thin veil of peace around their house. A veil that did not cover the distant shots or the craters; that did not hide the endless trail of people along the road: women in white mourning, weary men with old rifles.

Masood would walk down the rocky road to Nyala, till he was a spot of white on the horizon. She would already miss him as she watched from the trees and fingered her Taweez. The Ayatul-Kursi had protected her mother and grandmother. Masood said she was superstitious. She would still pray the Ayats to him as he walked down the road.

Amina does not remember Sudan or their home or warm asida. She likes Frosties for breakfast. This morning she sucked them till they were soft and showed them to

Nadia on the end of her tongue. She sighed and rolled her eyes when Nadia asked her to speak in Arabic, as if she expected her mother to know her new English words. But Nadia *is* learning. She wants to read bus tickets, road signs, newspapers. She needs to read the solicitor's letters and tribunal determination.

The bus driver is still in the car park. The woman next to Nadia closes her handbag, glances round, saying, *This is ridiculous!* She edges through the standing passengers and steps off the bus. Others follow, pushing to the front.

Amina is hot and fidgeting on Nadia's knee. Her school is not far. *Come on, Amina*, she says. *Let's walk.*

They are late for school, but Miss Miller has not yet taken the register. They slip into the classroom, trying to be quiet. Amina heads for the sandpit, but Nadia holds her back and hangs her bag on a peg.

Good morning, Amina, Miss Miller says. *Good morning Mrs Abdalla.*

Nadia smiles. *Good morning.*

Nadia usually slips away after the register when Amina is busy working. Miss Miller has favourite pupils but Amina is not one of them. At the beginning of the year Amina was silent, sullen. She did not 'participate in activities.' She bit Miss Miller's ankle. Now, Amina is in love with her voice. She screams and shouts and sings to Kylie.

Miss Miller seems agitated. *Sit down, everybody. Sit down*, she says. *They have gone*, she tells Nadia.

Sorry?

Fouad and Tijan. They have been detained. She turns to the class. *Quiet now. Register time.*

Nadia perches on a tiny chair next to Amina's. The school had a petition for the twins, Fouad and Tijan, which was sent to the Home Office. Nadia had carefully and slowly signed her name.

As Miss Miller says their names, each child stands and

says, *Good morning, everybody*. She pauses where Fouad and Tijan's names should have been. Amina is eying the sandpit; Nadia has to nudge her to answer. The register finishes and Amina runs over, plunging her hands into the pit, perhaps to feel the cold, moist sand around her fingers. She flings the sand in the air with a shriek.

Amina! Don't throw the sand! Come on, it's reading time.

Outside there is not enough air.

Nadia breathes, but still there is not enough air. She sits on the bench. The playground is empty; waiting for playtime and the children's steps. The wind is busy with crisp packets while shouts and laughter come from an open window. She can hear Miss Miller's voice:

Everybody on the carpet! Come on! Everybody sit on the carpet! Just leave those bricks, Muhammad. Leave them… what did I just say? On the carpet.

On the ground is a hair band. Red and pink and dirty. Dark hairs knotted round it. 'Hair band.' Amina taught her this word. She picks it up and twists it round her fingers. Other words. 'Sandpit.' 'Playtime.' 'Cheese Crisps.' She breathes slowly, in and out. 'Detained.' Amina will wonder where Fouad and Tijan have gone. Nadia does not know what she will tell her.

Last week, there was no air at the solicitor's. The office was dank, the fan chugging, sweat welling beneath her arms and inside her thighs. A fly clambered the window. Mr Williams wiped his pink, shiny forehead.

Tell Mr Williams he is a good man, she said to Amit. *A good man.*

Amit spoke in English to Mr Williams, who shook his head and talked for a while. Amit told Nadia that the appeal had been dismissed on both asylum and human rights grounds.

Why? She asked.

They don't believe you're a credible witness, Amit said. *There is no evidence of your husband's membership of the SLM. The adjudicator doesn't believe you would be persecuted by the militia if you returned to Sudan. Even if he was a member, you're just an innocent bystander.*

I'm telling the truth. They came and burnt my house. The Janjaweed took my husband from his work. She looked from the translator to the solicitor.

What do we do now?

Amit spoke and Mr Williams shrugged, folding her papers.

In the bus shelter's glass Nadia sees a woman in a red-orange khimar, the colour of clay, of midday heat. Beneath it her hair is thinning. She has massaged her scalp with oils, but still her hair has fallen out, leaving patches of skin. She tucks it over her ears and turns from the glass. She is almost glad Masood cannot see her long-shaped head, her dry skin.

Goodbye hair, Amina said when Nadia cut it off. *Goodbye hair.* Then she touched it in the sink and said, *Ooohhhh!* Hands deep in the hair, eyes full of her favourite game, she flung it in the air and around the bathroom, hair landing in little clumps.

Perhaps she will walk home. The street of houses is quiet, deserted almost, shaded by large trees. A breeze catches the heavy branches as she walks past the line of grey bins, spilling cans and cartons. She peers in one at the vegetable peelings and plastic wrappers.

She hurries through a number of streets and down Bromley Road, where there are no trees or greenery. The houses are smaller, red and identical. Her bedsit is on the second floor of a block of flats. Inside, the hall is dark and cool and the floor is scattered with past tenants' unopened letters. She steps over the letters and treads quietly up the stairs, thinking of how, about this time, her neighbours, Nagwa and Suhair, would visit for coffee and sometimes chat till lunchtime.

Closing the door, she pulls off the khimar and rubs her head. She opens the window and folds the blanket under the mattress. She tidies, picking up tissues and cups, Amina's socks and colouring book off the carpet. She hates this thick, dirty carpet, with its ugly orange swirls. She would prefer a floor she could sweep and wash.

She folds Amina's spare cardigan and carefully places it on their pile of clothes on the table. Next to the clothes, the book of fairytales lies open. Amina likes to tell her these stories. In them, people who disappear come back as swans, frogs, magical creatures, like the tales of ancestors from southern Sudan. She imagines Masood returning to her as a large white bird, soaring down from the sky.

Masood: stood awkward and stiff in his white shirt while their parents agreed to the marriage; his father spoke of Masood's job in Nyala and her father nodded and smiled. Nadia sat quietly, letting the khimar hide her face.

She carries the cups to the sink and washes the dishes, her fingers hurried, clumsy. She drops a bowl. A crack forms. She traces the crack with her finger and sees her hands are shaking. The bowl will fall apart when Amina pours her milk into it, holding the carton carefully with two hands.

The court documents and letters are in a ripped and tatty folder. Sitting on the mattress, she folds and unfolds the papers, the letters, the determination. The words – she traces her finger over the print, the strange round letters, the curving signature. She turns the brochure that opens the wrong way and lets the papers fall onto her lap. Amit's words, Mr Williams' words:

Unreliable witness… appeal dismissed… no proven breach of the 1951 Convention… removal…

Nadia finds the Taweez from under her blouse. The tiny silver book needs polishing; the grooves of the pattern have tarnished. She reaches behind her neck, unclasps the chain and gently takes out the paper. It is yellow and faded, the scroll barely visible.

She sinks back onto the mattress and thinks of how they were under the neem trees when the men came. The empty breakfast bowl on the ground and Amina in her arms. She saw them on the road in their cars, bouncing over potholes. They parked and entered the house, shouting to each other. She took Amina beyond the trees and lay in a crater, a deep hole blasted in the earth. She stayed there till sweat burnt on the back of her neck, till Amina cried and she heard the wheels skidding on the road.

It was the smell of smoke that made her climb out of the crater. Her house burnt easily, thick red flames eating the straw in the roof. They crouched under the trees till one of the neighbours ventured out and brought them water. It was hours till Masood's brother came and took them to Nyala.

Nadia rolls onto her front, feeling the cocooning warmth of her breath on the pillow and the Taweez digging into her palm. She can hear Indian music playing, then a phone ringing on the landing, someone speaking and the pattern of feet running down the stairs. There is a smell of spices; something good cooking. She would like gorraasa be dama, she would like to cook some for Amina when she comes home. It was Masood's favourite dish. He would roll up the flat gorraasa and catch the dripping sauce with his mouth.

She must get up and eat something. She cannot lie here all day. Her legs feel stiff and heavy as she stands. She peers into the fridge and wipes sticky stains from under the eggs she will cook for Amina's dinner. The milk carton is empty, but she will have the Frosties anyway. Nadia pours cereal into the cracked bowl and nibbles the Frosties one by one, tasting the crisp sweetness.

Down Duchy Road

THE WINTER I turned fourteen, we called on a woman down Duchy Road. I thought she was American, but she was from Salford though she'd lived in South Carolina. She was called Margery and had a flat in a two-storey block. The intercom didn't work and the door on the stairwell hung loosely. The stairwells smelt of wee, so I held my breath till I got to the top where it opened out onto a balcony.

It was the end of December. I was all wrapped up in my coat and hat, carrying a brown leather bag, heavy with my bible and *Watchtowers*. I was glad my school friends didn't live round here; I was terrified of them seeing me. I didn't know many of the kids down Duchy Road; they went to a different high school. They would watch, clustered around a lamp post, as if we were a sideshow, occasionally calling something out as we knocked on the doors. Only last week when I showed a neighbour *The Watchtower*, he'd said: 'Let me tell you something, darling. You should be getting out and having some fun.' I stared at him; he must have been crazy.

Margery was a return visit of John's. She took *The Watchtower* every month and invited us in for a chat and a brew. The first time John asked me to accompany him on the call I was shocked at how her cheek bones pierced through her skin and her shoulders stuck out like bent coat-hangers under her dressing gown. She was tall and had brittle, red hair wrapped around her head like a turban. She looked pleased to see us. I think she was won over by John's manners; with his brylcreemed, silver hair, his height and clean shaven appearance he seemed as if he was out of a black and white film. His wife was very ill with a kidney disease, and he hooked her up to a dialysis machine in his shed three times a week.

John and I sat on Margery's faded floral couch. I traced my glove over a stain and tried to breathe through my mouth; her flat smelt of stale cigarettes and beer and something rank.

Margery perched on the other chair and flicked through the magazine. 'A World Without War' was printed on a picture of a mushroom cloud set against a barren landscape. John asked her whether she thought a world without war was possible.

'Oh, I don't know,' she said. 'Haven't really thought about it. But it would be nice, wouldn't it?'

She looked at the contents page and muttered: 'Armageddon: The War to End All Wars', 'The Scrolls of Revelation', then placed it on the chair and turned to point to a framed photograph of a man in a blue uniform on the wall.

'That's my ex-husband, Jimmy, he's dead now. He was in the armed forces, you know.'

John peered over his glasses at the photo. Margery twisted in her chair and her shoulders began to shake. She looked ill, ghostly; her skin paper-thin, like an old woman's. I couldn't tell how old she was.

'Do you want some tea?' she asked and walked to her kitchen. I peered round her room, at the white bumpy wallpaper, peeling and yellowed with mould spreading in the corners. Books were piled on shelves, thrillers, Ruth Rendells; the type of novels my mum got from Height library. There was a wedding photo of a young woman with long red hair in a white dress holding onto the arm of the man in uniform.

'Karen, do you want to see if she needs any help?'

'OK.'

I tiptoed into the kitchen. 'Do you need any help?' I asked. She was pouring vodka into a mug. 'Here you are,' she said, handing me another. 'I don't have any milk, though.'

'That's OK. I can't drink milk.'

She smiled at me. The mug was wobbling in her hands. There was probably an article on alcoholism in a back copy of *The Watchtower*, with good advice. I'd look through my magazines when I got home.

We sipped our tea and John took out his bible and showed her Matthew 24: 6-8, while she squinted and followed the words with her finger. 'And you shall hear of wars, and reports of wars, but do not be troubled, for all these things must come to pass, but the end is not yet. For nation shall rise against nation, and kingdom against kingdom, and there shall be famines and earthquakes and pestilences in many places. All these are the beginning of sorrows.'

'There's more?' she said.

'But look,' John said, pointing to verse 14: 'And this gospel of the kingdom shall be preached in all the world for a witness unto all nations; and then the end shall come.'

I was thinking we could perhaps help her, make her some dinner, when there was a knock at the door. 'Margery!'

'It's Sid,' she said and hobbled to the hall.

Sid was a gnarled-looking man, even shorter than me. He had Co-op bags of cans and I could see the words 'Special Brew' through the plastic.

'This is my friend, Sid,' she said. 'This is John and his friend, what's your name, love?'

'Karen.'

She showed him her copy of *The Watchtower* and he raised his eyebrows and coughed. John must have felt awkward because he said it was time to be going.

A month after my first visit to Margery's flat, John's wife went into hospital. He asked me to call on Margery and told me to take a sister called Joan because I wasn't supposed to go into people's houses on my own. When we arrived, Margery was wearing the same pink dressing gown. She staggered as she walked and said, 'Come into the kitchen, dear. I'll make a brew.' Joan was left perching on the couch.

Margery leaned on the kitchen counter. 'You're not like them round here,' she said.

I heard that a lot. It bugged me, but I wasn't sure why.

Margery made the tea; she squeezed the teabag against the cup until the water turned dark tan. Then she poured in lots of milk and passed it to me. I didn't like to mention that I didn't drink milk, so I clasped it in my hands.

She said, 'I've been thinking about what John asked. And no, I don't think a world without war is possible. Look around you. There's no end to it.' She pointed around her kitchen, as if the evidence was in here. 'Not if there are Jimmys in this world.' She eased herself onto a wooden chair, saying, 'Let me tell you something.'

The mug was burning my fingers. I needed to put it down, so I tried to make room for it among the dirty glasses on the counter.

'I'll tell you something,' Margery said again. 'My husband, Jimmy, died.'

'I'm sorry,' I said.

'Yes. I know you are, love. That's why you do what you do. Well, he was my ex-husband. He died after I'd returned here. Operation Just Cause I think it was. I met him here, you know. Down Duchy Road. His aunt lived next door.'

'What was he like?'

'Sit down,' she said, so I sat on the hard chair. Margery went into the living room, saying to Joan, 'I'm just making a brew.' She came back in with the photo of her husband and handed it to me. He had short blonde hair and a friendly smile with dimples in his cheeks. The photo was in a wooden frame and behind the glass I could see it was yellowing at the edges. I perched it carefully on my knee on my *Watchtower*.

'Isn't he dashing in his uniform,' she said, switching on the kettle. 'There's nothing like a man in uniform.' She sat down on the other chair and crossed her legs. 'When he came to visit his aunt, I couldn't take my eyes off him. I leaned over the little wall that separated our front yards, blowing pink bubbles. He smiled as he knocked on the door. He had a lovely smile. Then his aunt opened the door. She gushed over him, "Jimmy, oh Jimmy. You're so handsome!"

'I waited outside, leaning and swinging on the gate, trying to hear what was happening. After a while, he came out and lit a cigarette.

'I was a looker then. My hair was long and brilliant red, like it was out of a bottle. But it wasn't. I did this thing, see.' Margery dipped her head forward. 'And it would fall over my face. Worked every time.

'The next day I leaned on the gate till he came out and I did the thing with my hair and he invited me for Sunday dinner with his family. I'd never been to dinner before. They had the roast all spread out like a king was visiting, and he sat at the head and carved the beef. His hand stroked my back as he passed me to get some glasses. It was like we were a couple.

'That evening he asked me to go to South Carolina with him. We got married in the registrar's on Albert Square, and then we flew to the States. I'd never been on a plane before. We went to visit his family. They were well off, very posh. Not like the ones down our way, and they weren't pleased with him marrying me. But we didn't care.' Margery had a sip from her mug and I tried the tea, but the milk tasted awful.

'We lived on post at Fort Bradley,' she said. 'We had our own quarters, all the married ones did. Two rooms. A bedroom and living room with a small kitchenette. We loved it and when we arrived we waltzed around the bed,' Margery said, smiling and doing a waltzing movement with her arms. Then she poured some vodka into her mug. 'But it didn't last,' she said. 'I wasn't cut out to be an army wife. The other wives were like they'd been trained. Sacrifice and chin up and all that. In our house, my mum didn't take any jip.

'I'll tell you this, love, I've always liked a drink. Who doesn't? And I was so bleeding bored. There was just nothing to do all day. The other wives organised afternoon vegetable carving and calligraphy circles, but none of that was my thing. I'd tidy up and then I'd walk round and round the base, with its neatly mowed lawns like a bowling green, watching as the men ran past to the training field. I'd try to smile and wave at the good-looking ones, but they weren't interested; I had Officer's Wife stamped all over me, which was depressing as hell. Sometimes, I'd see them punishing one of the new recruits. They'd spray him in the face with a hosepipe while all the others ran up to him and thumped him in the stomach.

'One day, it must have been three months in, I tried to go off base. The guard at the gate asked where I was going and for what reason. I said I had errands. He kept questioning me. Could I not get what I needed from the store on base?

'I told him I needed womanly things, which shut him up. I went to a bar in the town and ordered a whisky. Only one! On the way back, I picked up a bottle of Jim Beam. But at the gate, the guard searched my bags and found it. Jimmy was called down. When we got home, he closed the door behind him, saying, "Margery, you're a drunk. I can smell it on your breath." And I'd only had one. I was fuming. No one ever spoke to me like that back home.

'Anyway, I got myself dressed to go to a dinner party for the officers and their wives. He looked me over at the door and told me to put some lipstick on. Couldn't I make more of an effort?

'"I've made a bleeding effort," I said. He followed me back inside, saying all he wanted was for us to be happy together, but all I wanted was to lie in my own filth, drinking filth.

'We screamed at each other, shouting, hurling abuse. And then one of the officers knocked on the door, asking about the noise.'

Margery shifted on her seat. 'He couldn't understand. He'd grown up on an army base, and it was normal for him.' She paused, her mug in the air. 'For him it was a way of life.'

'So what did you do?' I asked.

'Nothing. I read all day. Anything I could get my hands on. Even Jimmy's Operation Manuals. I'd brought my bible, so I read that. I always loved the verse about the sparrows.'

I liked this verse too, so I said, 'Have no fear; you are worth more than many sparrows.'

'Yes.' Margery smiled. 'You are worth more than many sparrows.' She looked into her mug and swirled it around. 'Two years in,' she said. 'And it was the annual officer's ball. I remember trying on my dresses in the bedroom but they were all too big. Jimmy came in and said he'd get someone to take them in for me. One of the wives took in my favourite one. It was pink with blue flowers on it. I wore it for the ball and we were excited again, like when we first got married. He looked so handsome in his uniform, and as we entered the ballroom, he kissed my neck, murmuring he loved me and wished things could always be like this.

'People came up to Jimmy. The other officers shook his hand and the wives kissed him on the cheek and then they walked away as if I wasn't there.

'After a while Jimmy disappeared into the crowd and left me at my seat. I smoothed my dress and checked in my handbag while the officers and wives milled about me. A few of them began to dance in the middle of the room, then more joined in and I felt as if I had shrunk to a tiny figure on the floor and everybody was circling above me in a beautiful dance I couldn't follow. I looked up at them, thinking life would always be like this, seen from below.

'"Are you OK?" someone asked and I realised I had slipped off my chair onto the floor. I got up and staggered to the loo where I huddled in a cubicle, sipping from my hip flask, and when I felt able to, I dashed outside. The night was bright and smelt of one of those spring smells, you know... like honeysuckle. It was much nicer out there, so I walked towards the fence, and sneaked out through the guards' gate.

'I headed to the town, past the shops and the houses with their verandas. I remember it was late and no one was about, just a skinny dog with its paws on a bin, so I took the lid off for it to rummage inside. I headed to the river on the edge of the town, and walked along the bank, my sandals sinking in the marsh and reeds. I don't know what came over me, love, but I decided to tiptoe through the mud to the water's edge. I got it into my head that I was actually part of life on this base; I even had my own platoon. I was conducting an amphibian mission, like in one of Jimmy's manuals. An assault riverine operation. I know it sounds silly, but I thought I was the commander and I had to advance into enemy territory. My men were relying on me and I wouldn't let them down. I'd push myself to the limits, till beyond all endurance. I would cross the river.

'"I'm going in!" I shouted, wading into the water. "Follow me troops!" I was up to my thighs, my dress swirling around my legs. "To the other side, soldiers!" It was the mission to end all missions. We needed to get to the other bank and regroup. The water was thick and caressed my legs; the current nudging me, and then it pulled my feet off the riverbed and swept me away. But I wasn't frightened. I was drawn under the water and carried along, as if the river was protecting me.'

Margery paused and placed her mug on the counter. Underneath, I saw there were bags full of empty glass bottles. She leaned back in her chair and said, 'I woke up lying on a bank with a man leaning over my legs. I gasped, thinking he was the enemy, but he showed me a leech in his hand, saying, 'Look at the size of them!' It wiggled its red underbelly. I looked at where other leeches had attached themselves to my shins and ankles and screamed. My legs were covered in blood.'

Margery lifted her dressing gown. 'The scars are there, see.' But it was hard to tell because her skin was purple and scaly.

'The wounds bled for ages.' She covered her leg and took another gulp from her mug. 'I was taken to a local hospital and finally transferred to the one at the base. I remember Jimmy standing over my bed. "What were you doing?" he hissed into my ear. "Are you fucking insane? Were you trying to kill yourself?"

'But I couldn't explain about my little mission and that for the first time I'd had a role. Later that day he returned with the army doctors, and they said I needed psychiatric treatment for my drinking. I remember the blue of their uniforms surrounding me like dreary curtains around my bed.

'"Or," one of them said, "you could return to England."

'I asked to speak to Jimmy alone. The others left and he stood staring down at me, his arms by his sides as if he was on duty. I reached for his hand, thinking how awful I must look without any make-up and wild hair. "Come with me, Jimmy," I said. "Leave all this. Let's go to England and set up a new life there." He looked straight ahead, raised his hand in a salute and span on his heel, his patent shoes squeaking as he marched out of the room.

'I tell you I have never cried like I cried in that hospital bed. Then two weeks later I was put on a flight home. I don't know who paid for it, perhaps his family. But I'll tell you this.' She leaned forward, tapping me on the arm. 'I might like a drink, but it's in their blood. They love it, don't you see? There's no changing that.'

I looked at the *The Watchtower* in my hands, at the mushroom cloud on the cover, thinking of Margery stuck on that base, and one day it all being swept away by Armageddon, and there being no war anymore. Then I looked at the photo of Jimmy: his short, neat hair and kind smile; how every part of him seemed to shine, and how he had saluted her as he left.

I realised Joan was standing at the door and had been listening to the story; she surprised me because she didn't mention *The Watchtower*, she just said, 'Men!'

Margery nodded. 'They're not all like John are they?'

We agreed. Not many like John.

Margery took the *The Watchtower* from me and flicked through it. 'Is John coming again?' she asked, her voice brightening.

'He should be.'

When the Truck Came

I

WHERE THE ROAD curved around Mount Mikeno, the truck broke through trees that reached to a rim of clouds; then came the grinding of its tires on stones and mud.

'Look!' Japhet pointed and Lionel shaded his eyes to see. Perhaps it was a truck that delivered medicine, it was hard to tell. He had been told to hide from vehicles, but he squinted as its bonnet thundered through the redwood.

'Got you!'

A stone hit Japhet's arm, knocking his school books to the ground. 'Armel!' he cried as his friend ran up the road. He picked up his books - the pages reddened with dirt - and wrapped them in the cloth. He could see the truck nearing; its passengers visible as it veered round the track's bend. It was grey and green, with mud smeared over the sides. In the front were two men wearing khaki caps and sunglasses. The wheels span in the mud as it stopped in front of them and the doors swung open.

Hide from soldiers, his mother had warned, so Japhet shouted 'Run!' and sped into the undergrowth. He could feel the leaves falling behind him, but hands caught his shoulder and wrist. He was slung onto a shoulder and then thrust into the rear of the truck. Lionel and Armel landed beside him. The doors closed and the boys screamed into the blackness.

As they jolted along the potholed track, they huddled together; the air was hot and hard to breathe, so their crying

137

quietened to gasps and sniffs.

It was night time when they came to a stop and the doors were opened. Japhet struggled to sit up. Through the doors he could see they were in a clearing dotted with tents; men and boys sitting around fires, and behind them two more trucks.

'Welcome to the camp,' the soldier said, reaching towards him.

The next morning, Japhet woke up thinking he was back at home: his brother's elbow was digging into his back and his mother was about to start telling him to get ready for school. But opening his eyes, he saw only the blue of Armel's t-shirt, and the brown weave of the tent over him.

'Good morning, recruits.' A soldier crouched at the opening. 'I'm the Commander of this squadron. Commander Din.' The man had huge shoulders, a moon face with scarred cheeks and wore a red bandana around his forehead. 'You want to be soldiers, don't you?'

Japhet and his friends sat up, staring at the soldier.

'Don't you?'

'Oui,' said Japhet.

'No French. Only Swahili.'

Japhet nodded and the others did too.

'Good. Let's get started.'

The way he would remember it, years later, his schooling as a soldier began that first morning. He remembered them following Commander Din to the middle of the camp where a group of boys were standing next to a line of rifles. The other soldiers sat in front of their tents, eating bowls of rice and drinking from canisters.

'This is the most beautiful thing you will ever own.' Commander Din held a rifle in the air and then slipped it into the crook of his arm, positioning and pointing it at the boys. 'You must love it. Worship it. Sleep with it. Eat with it.' Then round he turned, again and again, falling into different positions, each time pointing the gun. He shoved it into Armel's face. Armel closed his eyes, his shoulders shaking. 'It is both your best friend and your enemy. Now. Kneel down in front of the guns.'

Japhet and the boys looked at each other.

'I said kneel down.'

They knelt down and stared at the row of guns on the ground, each pointing towards them.

'Now, bow down.'

They bowed down and Japhet strained to keep his face away from the ants crawling out of a hole in the earth.

'One of these rifles will be yours, if you show yourselves worthy. Now look at them. See how they shine in the sun? They shine because they are glorious.' Commander Din paused.

Japhet thought the rifles looked battered and old, not shiny at all.

'Stand up, recruits. I'm going to show you how to use them.' He handed a rifle to each boy. 'Support it with your left arm, plant it into your shoulder and hold your right elbow out like this.'

Japhet held his with both hands, as if he might drop and break it, but it was lighter and easier to hold than he'd imagined. He fitted it into his shoulder and lowered his face to the warm metal, poking out his right elbow.

'Everyone, put the gun in your shoulder,' Commander Din was saying. 'Good. Face to the side of the target, turn at the hips, and *fyetua*.'

Japhet pulled the trigger. '*Fyetua*.' Not knowing why, he licked the metal.

The next day another soldier called Lieutenant Leopold became their trainer. He was a tall, thin man with a narrow face and huge eyes like a mosquito; he used a whistle, which he blew into their ears. Lieutenant Leopold taught them how to pretend to fire in short bursts towards the lower part of the target. They pretended to shoot from waist height, when kneeling and when prone. They learnt how to strafe: short burst, run to the right, pause, short burst, to the left; always varying direction.

Japhet and the boys zigzagged across the clearing, firing, and going into a kneeling position. Finally, they were given live ammunition, and practiced sliding the magazine in and out of the rifle. Tilt the gun to the left, pull out the old magazine, slide in the new one, pull the lever, back to position and aim.

At the end, Japhet and the boys flopped onto the ground, panting in the sun. But there was more. The targets – sacks with melons for heads – were lined up, and one by one they fired their first shots. Shoulders were knocked back, some boys landing on the ground. Japhet managed to keep his balance and laughed as Lionel was sent flying.

Later that night, or it might have been another night, Commander Din and Lieutenant Leopold gathered the boys around the fire, ordering them to sit on the ground. 'Place your guns before you,' Commander Din said. 'I'm going to tell you a story.' He kneeled down and whispered, so they had to strain to listen. 'I'm going to tell you about the First Soldier.' He paused, and began again: 'Now, not many years ago and not far from here, our people were slaughtered. Their bodies filled the rivers until there was no room for the fish, until the river was a mass of bodies. The river flowed and wound its way until there was no water left, and only blood and bloated bodies passed along it. And then one day, the First Soldier came to the river, looking for something to drink. The First Soldier saw the blood and bodies and immediately tried to save them, but he couldn't because all he had was a raft, and the current of the river was fierce and the raft upturned. The bodies sailed on down the river, and the First Soldier had to hold onto the edge of his raft to stay afloat. He saw that the bodies had been hacked apart and they just kept coming. He could do nothing, as more and more of them floated past, down this river of blood. Then the First Soldier climbed out of the river and travelled upstream to where there were no more bodies so he could stop this river of blood at its source. The bodies had been killed with machetes, so he knew that the way forward was with a gun. One like this,' and Commander Din held up Japhet's rifle. 'One like this. To stop the river of blood. But the First Soldier couldn't do it on his own. He needed lots of soldiers. Soldiers like you with guns like this to stop the river of blood!'

He stood up, saying, 'Now. Take off your t-shirts and clean your guns.'

As the boys wiped their t-shirts up and down the muzzles, rubbing as hard as they could, Commander Din asked, 'Do you want to know who the First Soldier is?'

Japhet and the boys stared up at him. He paused, knelt down and whispered, 'The First Soldier is the General.'

'Today is a test.' Commander Din had divided them into two groups of six and handed out the rifles. Armel and Lionel were ordered to go in the other group, and Japhet watched as they disappeared into the trees. Commander Din then led Japhet and the five others through plantain bushes to a clearing where stumps of trees jutted from the ground.

Years from now, Japhet would remember the six of them still playing and teasing each other when the Commander told them: 'The one who turns, shoots and lives when I shout *fyetua* will be a soldier.'

Japhet looked at the other boys. He had sat with some of them a couple of times while they ate their bowls of rice. Sesu was older and already had broad shoulders, but Pelo and Eliki were younger. Commander Din split them into two lines. Opposite Japhet, Pelo was shaking and making a funny noise, like a goat bleating. Japhet tried to keep the gun steady in his arms.

'This row,' Commander Din said, pointing to Japhet and the two others. 'Keep a straight line, evenly spaced. Start walking. Pace, pace, Stop.' There was a pause, and in the middle of it, Japhet heard *fyetua*.

The burst of the rifle almost threw him off his feet as he span around. When he looked up, Sesu and the boy next to him were still standing, and the row in front of him were all lying on the ground. Eliki and the other boy were still, but Pelo was groaning, blood spreading through his t-shirt.

Commander Din dragged the standing boys by their hair and made them kneel on the ground in front of the injured boys, then he pushed their faces into the earth and blood. It smeared over Japhet's cheek and into his nose. 'Drink it.'

Japhet opened his lips till the blood and soil made him cough and heave.

'Now you are soldiers.'

Commander Din clapped them on their backs and allowed them to swig water from his canister. Japhet looked back at Pelo, but he had become still.

They were marched out of the clearing. Inside Japhet's head he could hear a noise, a kind of bleating cry. On and on it bleated in his head. He put his hands on his ears to stop it, but the noise was still there, as if a goat was trying to climb out of his ears.

'Hands down.' Commander Din clipped him on the back of the head. They walked through the rubber trees, while the soldier slashed at the trunks with a knife, white liquid bleeding from the stems.

At the camp, Japhet found Lionel sitting in the tent with blood smeared on his cheeks and chin. 'Where is Armel?' he asked, but Lionel just rubbed his ear, as if he too had a bleating noise in his head.

The next day the camp was packed away. The boys were given rolled-up tents to carry. As they marched, the goat noise still fluttered around his ears, so he practiced the numbers he had learnt at school. *Moja, mbili, tatu, nne, tano...* The numbers were his; something secret in his mind: *moja, mbili, tatu, nne, tano.*

Japhet and Lionel marched behind a boy called Omari, who had a large head and tiny, shrunken body. He was chatty and pointed out the roots they might trip over, as well as the lizards pretending to be branches. They marched to the shores of Lake Kivu, and for the first time Japhet saw how its water flooded the horizon. He looked for fish and things that might jump out and eat him, but he could see nothing; the water seemed dead.

They left the lake and walked on through the forest and mountainside, the teak and cedar trees stretching up above and blurring the sky. Japhet could see the glistening legs and necks of the boys and men in front, a long, snaky line walking on and on. Perhaps Armel was lying in a clearing somewhere; some other boy's face being pressed into a pool of his blood. Or he could be hugging his mother right now at the roadside where she had been waiting for him ever since that day.

Perhaps Japhet could escape with Lionel, and maybe Omari, but Commander Din had said that he would catch any boy who tried to escape and cut off his ear, as well as the ears of his friends. Japhet squeezed his earlobes. No boys had tried it yet.

In the mountains, they camped where Omari claimed the gorillas lived. Japhet could hear them calling in the forest, and the thud thud thud of them beating their chests. Some of the soldiers went hunting for bushmeat and brought back an okapi, its bluish tongue dangling from its mouth. But the next day they returned with a gorilla – its arms and legs tied to a pole – and set it down in the middle of the clearing. There were bullet wounds to its chest, as if it were a soldier shot in battle. Japhet and the boys lined up to feel the gorilla's fur and solid flesh. Japhet wanted to touch its face, but its eyes were closed as if it might wake and bite him, so he made do with stroking a hand, gently, like he would his mother's. They watched as it was skinned and carved up. He feared they'd have to press their faces into the blood, but they didn't as this was a different kind of killing; slices of meat were laid on stones to dry in the sun and chunks were stewed with vegetables in pots. The smell of the cooking made his stomach contract, and eventually they were given bowls of stew that were so hot and delicious the whole camp fell silent as they ate.

The gorilla's head was placed on a log and someone put a cap on it, as if it had joined the group. But when they moved on, the head was left behind. Japhet imagined the other gorillas finding the head and planning revenge. Omari agreed that the gorillas had their own army and fought soldiers in the rainforest.

They moved on every few days, walking up into the mountains and twice they saw a gorilla in the trees, as if it was watching them and plotting. The soldiers shot at it, but missed as it swung away.

The group camped in caves till they arrived at an old stone house in a clearing surrounded by eucalyptus trees. Japhet felt the black earth with the toe of his pump, and Omari, who seemed to know everything, said, 'It's the headquarters. We're going to meet the General.'

'I don't want to meet the General,' said Lionel.

'Don't say that, or they'll cut off your fingers and your nose.' Omari tried to grab Lionel's nose. 'Stop it!' Lionel cried, but they boys quietened when they saw soldiers sitting on the steps of the house.

The soldiers were wearing sunglasses and camouflage uniforms. One stood alone while Commander Din and Lieutenant Leopold lined the boys up in front of him. 'That's him,' Omari whispered.

The General surveyed the boys, giving them a broad

smile. 'You have been chosen,' he said, 'from Tutsi tribes to become Tutsi soldiers. *You* will protect the Tutsi. You know what has happened to many of our people. They have been murdered, slaughtered. We are here to make sure that doesn't happen again. We are going to fight the Interahamwe murderers as they try to pillage our country.' He walked down the steps. 'You are my sons,' he said. 'I am your father. We are a family and an army. Be good to me and I will be good to you.'

Japhet gaped at the men behind the General. They were now standing in a row with their hands clasped in front of them, wearing sunglasses and flak jackets stuffed with ammunition. The general raised his arms and said: 'You have proved that you can fight; and if you continue to prove this you will have a good life. Now get your uniforms.'

Bags of camouflage uniforms were brought out and handed round. The shirts were too big, but there were scissors to cut off the sleeves and belts to tie in the trousers. More soldiers arrived that afternoon. Young men and boys like them. The camp around the house was alive with noise and cooking and fires being made.

'I want to go home,' Lionel said, as they queued for their maize.

Japhet pulled at Lionel's ear. 'Don't say that.'

Lionel grabbed Japhet's arm. 'I want my mother,' he said, as if Japhet could get her for him. But Japhet's mother's face was an empty oval, a scary faceless face, so he punched Lionel's ear, and Lionel thumped him in the stomach.

There was a battle coming. The General said the Interahamwe were attacking villages in North Kivu. They came at night and crept into huts, cut people's hamstrings as they slept, and then waited till the morning to kill them. He showed on his leg where the hamstring was.

While they were practicing with their rifles, Commander Din pushed them into two groups. Japhet and five other boys were put together, while Lionel and Omari remained where they were. When everybody was separated, Commander Din said, 'Come with me,' pointing to Japhet's group. 'You're ready to be soldiers.' He waved the other group away. 'You're staying behind.'

Japhet didn't want to go on his own. Not without Lionel or Omari. The boys in Japhet's group pulled at their hands and kicked dirt with their shoes. Sesu was crying even though he was taller than the rest.

They marched for a couple of hours till they arrived at a wide clearing, where men were lying on the ground with bloodied rags wrapped around their arms and legs, and boys ran back and forth with water. Smoke wafted above the trees and from somewhere came the patter of machine gun fire.

As Japhet and the other boys walked past the bodies and towards their first battle, Japhet counted: *moja, mbili, tatu, nne, tano*… There was a rushing in his stomach, so he ran to the undergrowth and pulled down his trousers.

A moment later he appeared with his gun at his shoulder. *Moja, mbili, tatu, nne, tano* he counted, as he walked towards the rubber trees and the rising smoke.

II

In those years, what Japhet did became black patches in his mind. He didn't return from his first battle; he was sent on other missions with Commander Din, who commended his fighting as they ranged through Kivu and patrolled the border of Rwanda, protecting villages against the pillaging of government troops and the Mai-Mai. The government's soldiers were underfed, wild-eyed waifs – Japhet was glad he hadn't become one of them. At some point Commander Din died, and he was replaced by other commanders while Japhet moved up through the ranks to become a lieutenant, working on recruitment and collecting commissions from the General's diamond mines. The diamonds went towards supplies, food and arms, but now that Japhet had been appointed to the General's personal brigade, he held onto a few for himself: tiny, glittering things like the numbers in his head; something for him.

Japhet turned over in his tent, listening to the sounds of the night; the birds and crickets. He was glad an oil lamp was on in the clearing outside the General's house. It was the first time he had been back to Headquarters in years, and he'd had that dream again about his home: of dark, cool passageways and earth under his bare feet; rooms that were dank and cold, walls that hardened into stone as he stumbled over things on the floor.

He lay there, amid the drone of insects and uneven snoring, till the camp woke with the dawn. Then it was the clatter of pans and fires lit for breakfast. One of the new boys, Moise, brought him ashanti chicken with yams. When he had finished, he sent the boy for more.

Japhet had found two boys at the edge of a logging camp, watching as slash was burned to clear the ground. He hadn't seen the other workers for all the smoke, but he could hear a chainsaw buzzing somewhere. Japhet and another lieutenant crept up behind the trees to ambush them, but when they were close, the two boys didn't run. They turned – woodchip stuck to their hair and dust on their t-shirts – and walked towards them, their hands in the air, as if they had been waiting for Japhet to arrive.

Japhet allowed the two boys to ride to the camp in the front of the truck, but when they did the shooting game, one ran so Japhet had to shoot him himself. This boy, Moise, shot his opponent in the head without blinking, then walked over to see if he was dead, prodding him with his foot.

Japhet had realised that the new boys had to go through fear till there was nothing left. It was a rite of passage. When they came out the other side they were pliable and would do anything he ordered.

'I want to talk to you.'

The General was kneeling at the opening of his tent, a cap pulled low over his forehead, his sunglasses in his hand. Japhet scrambled out, blinking in the sun.

'I've heard good things about you,' the General said, patting Japhet on the back. 'Come inside.'

Japhet had never been inside the house, but there was something about the cold, dank passageway and about the air that reminded him of his dream; this was the house he had been running through. He followed the General into a dark room with shuttered windows, which the General unlocked and pushed open. There were wooden chairs and a table with papers, maps and a phone. The General sat down, crossing a leg over his knee. 'Sit,' he said. Japhet sat on the other chair. The General had not changed; he wore the same camouflage clothing and his skin was smooth and clean. 'Are you ready for a promotion?'

'Yes.'

'Good. I'd like you to be one of my bodyguards.'

At dusk, Japhet went on post, joining the other guards sitting on the steps. One of them was familiar. Japhet stared at him and then said, 'Omari.'

The man raised his eyebrows. 'Japhet!'

They laughed. Omari said he'd been one of the General's guards for six months now. Japhet sat beside him as he and two others showed Japhet how to play a game with cards. He surprised them by saying the numbers in French. They raised their glasses to this, nervously, and as he drank the thick, brown liqueur he knew he could never say the Swahili words out loud; they were his numbers.

He went to lean on the veranda railing, staring at the darkness, the tips of the trees, and the vast rainforest beyond. The French numbers reminded him of his school books: how he'd dropped them on the road, the covers dusty with red dirt.

Omari stood beside him. He hadn't grown like Japhet had, but he had scars on his face and arms.

'It's a good life here,' Omari said. 'Plenty of food, drink, you're away from the fighting. We get the pick of the girls.'

Japhet ran his finger over the splintered wood of the railing. 'Lionel?' he said.

'He escaped soon after you left. They did this to me for it.' Omari pointed to his ear, which was a whole surrounded by lumps of scarred tissue.

'Did he go home?' Japhet asked.

'Maybe he did.'

'Which newspaper are you from?'

'*Le Monde.*'

The journalist was slight, with brown curly hair and pink, mottled skin. The General met him on the veranda and they drank coffee in the late afternoon, while Japhet and the other guards sat on the steps, listening to them speak in French. The journalist, who had shaken hands with all of them, said, 'General, what I want to know is, why have you been fighting for so long?'

The general took off his sunglasses. 'Young man, issues of conflict and peace are often complex. We work in a web of relationships, each reacting to the other. Many terrible things have been done to the Rwandan Tutsis as well as the Congolese in the North East. I am fighting for them all, to protect them and to protect the land itself. Do you know how many people want to rob the DRC of its wealth? That is all the foreigners have done. This house,' he said, waving to the building, 'Was the home of Belgian colonists. They have come and they have taken. Our diamonds, our minerals, our forests, our bodies. Do you have a phone?'

'Yes,' the journalist said, getting out a slim mobile. Japhet and Omari peered over to look at it. The journalist smiled and passed it to them to examine.

'Eighty-five percent of the world's coltan ore is from the DRC. Your phone is probably made from it. Corporations invest in keeping this country unstable so they can plunder our resources without remunerating our people. That is a fact.'

The journalist smiled, as if he'd heard about this speech before. 'Do you want to trade with them?'

'No. Never. I am here to protect the people and the country from them, as I am here to protect it from other rebel groups. That is my role. The people ask *us* to protect them. The government in Kinshasa of that dummy Joseph Kabila is a proxy government. Their forces pillage and commit atrocities. Even the UN knows what the government's troops are doing, but they are not brought to justice, are they? The Hague is not interested in them, is it?'

'You are very educated,' the journalist said.

The General shrugged. 'I attended university in South Africa, but everything I need to know is here. I will fight to my dying day for my countrymen. Write that in your paper.'

III

The days were hazy, passing without the regularity of being in the field; the training, the marching. The General seemed to be in contact with all his commanders by phone, and each of the five platoons would visit regularly and show off their new recruits, but there seemed little for Japhet to do.

Over cards and cigarettes, Omari and Japhet joked that they should get wives and make their own recruits, but Japhet thought that if he had a wife, he would carry her off to somewhere safe. He'd take her home. This thought came to him like a radio broadcast from somewhere far away; tinny and faint; a wife, and with this, the thought of home, of Chada. That was the name of his village. Chada. He had heard it in a dream, *his* dream, where shadowy passageways led to hidden rooms that went on and on. As he crept through the rooms he found members of his family lying on the floor, an uncle, an aunt, as if asleep, and in other rooms he found smaller bodies piled up.

Japhet woke in one of the rooms in the stone house, and with it the chill of the dank passageways. His skin was slick with a cold sweat, as if he had a fever. The other guards were sleeping in their blankets. He got up and went outside to warm himself in the sun, but he stopped at the door. The General and Omari were sitting on the veranda steps, and the General was saying, 'You've always been loyal, Omari.' Japhet went inside to the kitchen. He sat at the table, trying out the sound of his home on his tongue. 'Cha-da.'

He opened the window's shutter. Chada was out there, somewhere: houses and huts, with a church, but no school because the school was in the next village. He remembered then, when the truck came. He remembered it all: Lionel, Armel and he walking on the road, his books falling to the ground; running into the undergrowth and being picked up. He remembered licking the rifle and touching the gorilla's springy flesh; his face being pressed into blood and dirt, the sound of gunfire as he walked towards his first battle; the goat bleating and Lionel saying, 'I don't want to meet the General'; the platoon of gorillas in the forest and the head left on a stump, wearing a cap and its lips counting, *Moja, mbili, tatu, nne, tano.*

Fyetua! the gorilla's head orders. *Fyetua!*

The other guards were cheerful over breakfast. There had been victories in the area and they were moving north.

'Where to?' Japhet asked.

'Chada.'

'Chada,' Japhet said. Of course!

'There's a lot of Mai-Mai there,' Omari said. 'The

General wants some fun.'

'I know that place. Where is it?'

'Ha! I know.' Omari explained they would go northeast towards Lake Kivu and then it was north to Mount Mikeno.

That evening, he slipped into the guards' room and packed his stash of diamonds in his breast pocket. He would go with just his rifle and knife. If he got a head start, he could be a day ahead of the troops and warn his village. They would have to flee. They might not want to know him. Not after being a soldier. Perhaps Lionel was there, and Lionel could explain.

He could see his home clearly now: his mother cooking with a pot on a small fire; other women sitting with her, laughing and cooking maize; his little brothers chasing each other; the walk to school in the next village; the classroom under an awning and all the children writing their numbers on paper.

Omari and the other bodyguards were sitting on the steps, playing cards, and the General was in his office. Japhet slipped into the kitchen and pushed the shutter of the window open.

'Japhet.'

The General was standing in the doorway. 'Omari is worried about you; he asked me to have a chat. Here.' The General offered him a cigarette from a silver holder. Japhet stepped forward and took one, letting the General light it for him.

'You're a quiet one, Japhet, but you're a good soldier. I've seen you grow. I remember you from being a young boy. People don't know this. But I remember every one. Everyone matters.'

He didn't know whether to hold the General's gaze or to look into the distance as they were supposed to do on duty, so he focused on his cigarette. The General inhaled and then said, 'Do you know what I have done for you?'

Japhet finished his cigarette and crushed it with his boot.

'I gave you a purpose. This country is devastated. It has been pillaged and plundered for a hundred years, more, and the world has left us to rot. But we will make it great. We will. You and me. We will make it a great country. One for Tutsis to be safe in, for all people to be safe in. That is what we are fighting for.'

The General held his cigarette in the air, and his other arm was raised, as if he was addressing a group of new recruits.

But Japhet didn't know what the General was talking about. All he could think of was the rooms and endless passageways. The walls were thinner now, made of mud and straw. He was trying to find his way out, but he couldn't because he was tripping over the bodies; the corridors were piled with the rotting bodies of men and boys, shredded by machine guns. He was climbing over the shrivelled legs of boys, stepping on their skinny backs as the passageways filled with water and the bodies floated around him.

The General was watching him with narrowed eyes. He exhaled and seemed to be about to carry on with his speech, so Japhet stepped forward, slipped his knife from its sheath and flicked it into the General's ribs. The General lunged at Japhet – his own knife grazing Japhet's neck – and then he collapsed, his head hitting the stone floor. He gasped and coughed as Japhet grabbed his rifle and climbed through the window. From the back of the house, he ran for the trees and did not stop till he was well into the forest. The cut wasn't deep, but he ripped the arm off his shirt and tied it around his neck.

He ran till morning, then he slept and ran on for four days and nights, past Lake Kivu and the mountains to the north, past the blackened stumps of trees and the smoking head of a volcano, running and running, until, on the fifth day, there was something about the light and how the track curved, and the deep peaty smells of the undergrowth that seemed to belong to him. As did the banana trees like the ones he used to climb up, with Lionel waiting below to catch the bunches as they fell.

He knelt down to smell the red earth. He was on the road he'd been on when the truck had come. The trees rose thick and high above him and in that moment he could picture that truck once again speeding around the bend. Only this time he and his friends would have rifles and they knew how to strafe and run and strafe again, shooting from the waist, zigzagging in perfect formation.

Japhet walked down the road till he saw a group of huts in the distance. Then he hid in the undergrowth to see who was about. The village had grown; there were larger huts and more stone buildings, but there were no fires burning, no smoke or noise. There was no one there at all. Chada was deserted. He crept around, wondering which hut had been his home. From the tracks, the scattered pots and wood, the lame goat tied to a pole, he could see his people had left quickly. They must have fled to refugee camps. He untied the goat, so it could run off into the forest, but it only hobbled a few paces, stopped and watched him crouched on the ground, fingering the red earth.

After a while, Japhet walked back to the road. He could hear a truck in the distance, no, maybe two or three vehicles; the sound of their wheels spitting gravel and mud. He stood and shaded his eyes, squinting at the sight of a bonnet bursting through the redwood.

Crystal Night

'"THE JEWESS ENDANGERS the institute." That's what Kurt Hess has been saying.' Otto Hahn was pacing back and forth in front of Lise's desk. She ignored him and continued writing up the results; she'd already heard what Hess had said, what they were all saying about her.

Otto leant on her desk, perspiration pricking his forehead. 'Lise. Are you listening? I lost my nerve and talked to Horlein about this foolish situation. Something needed to be done about you and Hess.'

Lise dipped her pen in the ink. She couldn't account for their results with thorium any more than she could with uranium. The reaction of fast neutrons with thorium resulted in three different decay series. It didn't seem possible.

'Horlein said you may have to resign. Perhaps you could stay on in an unofficial capacity. He even said you may have to vacate your apartment!'

'What?' Lise pushed back her chair and placed her hands on her knees. 'I don't know why you had to say anything to Horlein at all.'

'I'm sorry, Lise, I'm worried about the Institute.'

'I know you are.' She pretended to sort through her papers till Otto had left the room and his footsteps had disappeared down the corridor. She couldn't believe he had spoken about her. The air in her office felt still and empty; she was alone in this institute. Utterly alone. She couldn't just sit there, so she gathered her coat and walked through the grounds towards her apartment, picking her way over the patches of snow. The trees and greenery were usually calming and blocked out the street vendors and trams of Dahlem, but she could still hear a parade.

She had managed to hold on till now at the Institute, putting up with the party members vying for her position and twittering on about the greatness of Aryan Physics, but now Austria had been annexed and for this she was supposed to gracefully resign after thirty years? As if she had done something wrong?

Her boots sank in a deep patch of snow, so she lifted her skirts and stood under a tree where the grass was dry. Here, she took her Austrian passport out of her bag and flipped through the pages. This document was defunct, like an outdated theory.

She was, in effect, back where she had started in 1908 when the entire Kaiser Wilhelm Institute for Chemistry had been off-limits to women. 'What if you set fire to your hair in the laboratories?' Emil Fischer had asked, not unkindly. It had been dear Otto who had suggested that they work together in the old carpenter's shop in the basement, where he had set up equipment to measure radiation. It had a separate outside entrance, so she could go to a restaurant down the street to use the toilet. She had liked Otto immediately; his sociability and willingness to work with a woman. Even his upturned moustache. They had always worked well together. In 1918, with Otto returning from the front and Germany in chaos, while it seemed as if the crazy socialist ideas of the Spartacists would take hold, Lise and Otto had discovered the radioactive element protactinium, the element just before uranium in the periodic table. Now the race was on to explain various strange observations that seemed to indicate still heavier elements – out in the mysterious zone beyond uranium: the 'transuranes'.

She found a packet of cigarettes in her bag, lit one and leaned against the tree. She could have left when Albert and

everyone else had, five years earlier, but Otto had promised
her that this department would be different, they could keep
working together despite the race laws, and she'd supposed
things would calm down eventually. They had even
managed to get a small stipend for Fritz Strassmann to join
their team. He had been unemployable and virtually starving
after refusing to join National Socialist organisations.

But now, Otto, dearest Otto, had in effect kicked her
out.

In June, Lise was sitting in her room in Hotel Adlon, which,
she had told herself, was only a temporary adjustment. To
make do, she had turned the dressing table into a desk, with
her books piled in front of the three-way mirror. She was
re-reading Bohr's article on 'Neutron Capture and Nuclear
Constitution' in *Nature*, and still trying to interpret the results
with uranium, when Carl Bosch, president of the Kaiser
Wilhelm Society, phoned.

'Lise,' Carl said. 'I've asked the Ministry of Education
about getting you a passport.'

'I'm sure that won't be necessary...'

'Well, in any case, they're determined not to give you
one. Let me read it to you.'

16 June 1938
'It is considered undesirable that well-known Jews leave
Germany to travel abroad where they appear to be
representatives of German science, or where their names
and corresponding experience might demonstrate their
inner attitude against Germany. Surely the KWG can find
a way for Frau Prof. Meitner to remain in Germany even
if she resigns, and if circumstances permit she can work
privately in the interests of the KWG. This statement
represents the particular view of the Reichsführer-SS and
Chief of the German Police in the Reichsministry of the
Interior.'

Lise scribbled it down in shorthand. 'Well, perhaps I can just keep working here in an unofficial capacity.'

'You must listen to me, Lise. I've spoken to Coster and Bohr and they are both adamant you must leave. They're making enquiries for you. I thought about speaking to Himmler himself, but Bohr advised against it.'

'No, please don't speak to him.'

Lise replaced the phone and dabbed at her face; the days were getting hotter and her situation more and more ridiculous. What did they mean? Her 'inner attitude against Germany?' After she had lived here all her adult life. Anyway, she'd converted to Protestantism when she was a girl. Everyone knew that. Since she was only allowed to work in an 'unofficial capacity' their team had made little progress, and the transuranes seemed to be even more of a puzzle. Otto and Strassmann were still bombarding uranium with neutrons, and trying to detect the new elements forming in the precipitate. It was well known that if a neutron was captured, the new element created was unstable and quickly decayed to a lighter element, but there seemed to be more than one species forming. Curie and Savitch had failed to interpret the so-called '3.5 hour activity' they had detected, eventually claiming it must be a transurane. Lise and Otto had nicknamed it 'Curiosum', and privately doubted that it was any such thing.

And here she was stuck in this airless hotel room. She tried to open the window, but the latch was stiff, and outside there was another rally in Pariser Platz. Above the marching soldiers and cheering crowd, Brandenburger Tor shone a beautiful, gleaming white in the sunshine, despite the swastikas hanging limp between the columns.

On the 12th July, the plan was to pretend it was a normal day. Lise worked till eight in the Institute, correcting a young colleague's paper, then she went to Otto's to pack what she could into two small suitcases and stay the night. Everything had been arranged by Dirk Coster and Niels Bohr. She wouldn't be going back to Hotel Adlon, though she hadn't checked out.

Bohr had tried to find her a position in Copenhagen, but he'd said it was quite impossible on account of the great number of foreigners already working in the institute; he'd already found places for numerous refugee scientists, including Lise's nephew, Otto Robert Frisch. Coster was trying to raise funding for a position in Amsterdam, but Lise had heard there was a new physics institute in Stockholm. The director, Manne Siegbahn, seemed open to offering her some kind of position. Perhaps she could be of some use there.

Lise was in Otto's spare room, packing her few summer clothes. She hadn't been able to bring her books and journals, her notes and writing materials, but hopefully they could be shipped later on. She closed the cases and sat wearily on the bed.

'Lise, I've got something for you,' said Otto, coming to sit beside her. 'Here, it was my mother's.' He placed a small blue box in her hand in which sat a diamond ring. 'Edith and I want you to have it. In case you need to sell it.'

'I'm sure I won't need to do that.' Lise slipped it on her finger. 'But it's beautiful. Thank you.'

The ring – a simple gold band with a small diamond – seemed out of place on her fifty-nine year old hand. Even so, she would wear it.

In the morning, Lise struggled to climb onto the packed train at Lehrter Bahnhof. She was wearing her ring under her glove and carrying a suitcase in each hand. She squeezed down the corridor till she saw Coster sitting by the window in one of the compartments. Her seat was opposite. A woman with a small boy pushed in with a suitcase, which Coster lifted onto the top rail. Then he turned to help Lise with hers. He smiled, but didn't say hello; they weren't supposed to speak till they were safely over the border, so Lise sat down with her handbag and tried to make herself comfortable, but under her dress and coat she had a cold sweat and her mouth was dry.

On the other side of the carriage, Coster looked pale, as if he had developed a fever; he must be as nervous as she was. He reached up and wiped his forehead with a handkerchief, then gave her a quick wink and closed his eyes. Next to him, the woman laid her boy's head on her lap and stroked his hair.

As the train drew out of Berlin and into the countryside, Germany started to look like it used to – fields growing sunflowers and rye, then valleys dotted with cottages – until they reached the stations when swastikas swarmed into view again.

Lise took the newspaper from her bag and flicked through the pages. She hardly read the papers these days; they were full of ridiculous ideas. However, on her final day in Germany she'd wanted to know what she was leaving. There was more of the usual nonsense: pages and pages on the mass rallies:

The Jewish Problem is the Background to World Politics
To a tightly packed Vereinshaus, Suendermann highlighted the fact that recognition of the Jewish threat must be spread to all the nations. He added that no people or leader longs for war, but we know that the question 'peace or war' is not to be decided by the will of the nations but through the might and influence of the Jews. Only when domination by the Jews is done away with will world peace be possible...

Lise sighed, dropping the paper on the seat beside her. People would see reason, that all this was foolish nonsense, she was sure of it. Coster was staring out the window, while the woman was fussing over her little boy. Lise rested her head in her hand and focused on the rhythm of the train, its soothing whoosh and chug, as if she was only visiting Gusti and Jutz in Vienna and she would return in a few days to the laboratory.

She woke to the train halting at a station and the sounds of voices. They were at the border town of Nieuweschans, and the woman had gone.

'Look,' said Coster.

Lise peered out of the window to see uniformed Nazi officers and Dutch border police getting on the train.

'Don't say anything. Just show them your entrance permit.'

Lise didn't have a passport or a travel visa, only a permit from The Hague that Coster had obtained for her. The day before, he'd travelled to meet the border police and they had assured him a permit would be enough. From the corridor, she could hear the barking commands of police checking documents. Coster was watching the compartment door and turning his passport over in his hands. Then they were crowding into their compartment, the Dutch policeman gesturing for her document, and the German soldier saying 'Heil Hitler!' over his shoulder.

'Heil Hitler!'

The Dutch policeman handed her permit back, and gestured for Coster's.

Lise stared straight ahead till they reached the University town of Groningen, breathing in short sharp breaths.

There was no reception in the foyer of Stockholm's Nobel Institute for Experimental Physics and no one to speak to. The new building was white and vacant; Lise's shoes echoed on the smooth floors, and the foyer was a gaping space with several corridors stretching outwards. At the end of one were two men in white coats. 'Excuse me?' Lise called, but they disappeared up the corridor, leaving an echo of their Swedish voices. She clenched her hands at her sides and followed the signs to Manne Siegbahn's room, peering through windows into empty laboratories and rooms that didn't seem to have any function at all.

The place seemed deserted and Siegbahn wasn't in his office, so she walked round and round the corridors and then back down the hill, where she caught a tram to her hotel in downtown Stockholm. Her room was narrow, with murky white walls, a bed and washstand. There wasn't even a desk where she could work.

She sat on the bed and began writing to her sister, Gusti Frisch, in Vienna. In the morning, she would apply for visas for Gusti and Jutz, though it was only a precaution, really.

Lise finally met Manne Siegbahn two days later. He was rushing down the hall with papers in his arms – a grey, tired looking man, hardly the youthful physicist she'd worked with in Lund, nearly twenty years before.

'Prof. Siegbahn.'

'Yes? I'm sorry, you are...?'

'Professor Meitner.'

'Frau Meitner, how wonderful. We meet again. Good, good.'

'I was wondering where I was to work. Which laboratory space I may use.'

'Ah... yes. Well, I can find you somewhere, of course. I'll be right back.' Siegbahn hurried into a room and closed the door. She sat on the chair in the corridor, perching her bag on her knee and shivering in her dress. Finally, a young assistant came out, saying, 'I'll show you to your room.' He couldn't have been more then twenty-five and spoke to her as if she was a student.

He led her down the stairs to a small, narrow room, holding out his hand to indicate she should enter.

Inside, there were tables and empty bookshelves. She placed her bag on a desk and looked at the assistant. But he had already gone.

By September, Lise still hadn't managed to get hold of any equipment for her laboratory. No counters, sources, capacitors or ammeters. Not a fraction of what, for years, she'd taken for granted in Berlin. For an institute in experimental physics, it was quite impossible to do any experiments at all. The days were growing chilly and she was constantly cold in her summer clothes. On an assistant's stipend – the kind of wage she had received thirty years previously – she had only enough to cover limited food and travel. Her pension and bank account had been frozen in Germany, and it was proving difficult for Otto to send her belongings. In her letters, she pleaded with him to send her the rest of her library. 'I hope it is understood that I will receive my journals, card-files, slides, diagrams of my experimental apparatus and so forth,' she wrote. But hitch after bureaucratic hitch came up.

Thankfully, there was an overnight mail from Stockholm to Berlin, so she could keep in touch with Otto and her lawyer. Lise's mail was delivered to her room every morning. It seemed cruel that the most treasured moment of her day should come so early. She would lie in bed, waiting to hear the shuffle of the porter placing the envelope on the mat outside her door. Then she'd reach for the spare blanket, wrap it around her and dash to retrieve the envelope and climb back into bed. It was still dark when the post arrived; she was dreading winter when it went dark by three in the afternoon.

At the university she would set up a few separation experiments and stare at them, but it was no use. She needed a chemist to work with, a source of neutrons, and a Geiger counter for her to do anything remotely like the work she was doing in Berlin. If only she had organised her departure earlier and been able to bring some equipment with her.

She would listen as someone walked past her office, their shoes echoing up the hallway. There was hardly anyone in the Institute other than the four young physicists in Siegbahn's group, but she wasn't invited to participate. They would blink at her when she attempted to speak to them in Swedish, so that she stumbled over her words, nervous, as if she were a shy young woman again.

Back when she had first arrived at the Kaiser Wilhelm Institute and they were only just letting women into universities, she'd walk next to Otto, fearful of everyone who spoke to her. The chemistry students ignored her, greeting Otto with 'Good morning Dr Hahn,' as if by not acknowledging her existence they could make her go away. It was the same when Siegbahn stared over her shoulder. He had done the honourable thing in helping her, but he didn't want a woman in his laboratories.

She shouldn't have come to this institute. It had been a mistake.

On quiet days, when there nothing to be done, she would re-read Otto's letters.

25 October 1938
Dear Lise,
Despite dreadful weariness, I want to answer your letter. Toward the end of last week a new paper by Curie and Savitch about the 3.5 hour substance appeared. We are now working on reproducing the experiments and we do now believe in its existence. According to Curie's results, we have found the substance, perhaps even better than Curie and Savitch. The properties do in fact appear to be remarkable. But we still have to identify it. (Perhaps a radium isotope has something to do with it. I tell you this only with great caution and in confidence). A great pity

you are not here with us to clear up the exciting Curie activity!

A great pity indeed. She could see Otto and Strassmann in their laboratory on the first floor of the institute, completely silent as they lifted the lead shielding between the tube of beryllium-radium powder and the uranium compound. The source would be inside a paraffin wax cylinder, in order to slow down the neutrons, and for a whole minute, the powder would shoot neutrons at the uranium. Otto would keep his eye on the clock, and after this minute, slide the lead shutter down to stop the bombardment.

The uranium would be dissolved in hydrochloric acid. Then the work of separating these substances from the solution would begin.

Lise carefully folded up the letter, and placed it in the envelope. She had replied to this letter saying she had obtained the Curie paper and found many statements hard to understand. The 3.5 hour substance was very intense and she wondered why they hadn't found this substance in thorium when they'd repeated the Curie experiment last January.

She opened Otto's reply and smoothed back her hair.

30th October 1938
Dear Lise!
With thorium as carrier we could not find it. It isn't thorium of course. At most, thorium is gradually produced from it. If anything definite turns up next week, I'll write again.

This reply had been so brief and enigmatic that she had written asking him again how the experiments were going. She had hoped that after thirty years of work and friendship together in the Institute, he could at least tell her what was happening there. But his most recent letter had been the most puzzling of all. Otto and Strassmann no longer seemed to think there was a single 3.5 hour activity, but a number of different activities involving radium.

2nd November, 1938

Dear Lise,

I am certainly not keeping secrets from you about work or Institute matters. We really could not say anything definite about the 3.5 hours substance in two weeks, despite working day and night, when Curie has been at it for 1 Ω years. We are now almost convinced that we are dealing with several - or 2 or 3 - radium isotopes, which decay to actinium. Perhaps we can feel sure enough by Sunday so that on Monday we can write a letter to *Naturwissenschaften*. Because the finding of radium is really so interesting and improbable that we would like to publish it before Curie gets to it, and before she hears of it from anyone else. That was the reason I wrote to say that you should please not say anything about it.

Naturally, we would like it very much if you could think about the situation, how an alpha transformation can come about, probably also with slow neutrons and at the same time produce several radium isomers.

Love Otto.

On the 13th November, Lise stood in Copenhagen Central Station, hugging herself against the wind that whipped down the platform. It was barely seven and there were only three other people waiting for the express train from Berlin. Niels Bohr had managed to organise her permit to come to Copenhagen while Otto was visiting to give a lecture. She was wearing the shawl, hat and thick underwear that Margrethe Bohr had given her, but the cold inside her, the shivering, the clenching of her stomach wasn't because of the wind. Yesterday, Bohr had showed her a newspaper, and translated from Danish that Jewish property had been destroyed all over Germany and the former Austria. Synagogues ransacked; shop windows broken, people had been attacked and thousands of Jewish men imprisoned. And as Lise looked at the photo of broken windows on the front of the paper, she knew it wasn't the spontaneous event they claimed it was; it had been planned. It was a strategy.

All morning, Lise had tried to phone her sister in Vienna, but the operator had not been able to put her through. That afternoon, she hadn't gone to the colloquium at the university, but instead walked round Copenhagen till she was lost in the backstreets, and then returned to Bohr's to find a telegram from Gusti saying that her husband Jutz had been arrested and sent to Dachau.

Otto's train drew into the platform. The carriage was packed and Lise strained to see him as the passengers brushed past her. Finally, there he was with his wonderfully familiar moustache under a brown trilby. They hugged, her head against his coat. 'Lise,' Hahn said, pulling back to look at her. 'You're a bag of bones!'

'Four months! It's been four months!'

They hurried to Otto's hotel, where they took breakfast in the dining room. He picked up his napkin and then put it down again. 'You've heard, haven't you, what's happened?'

'Yes.'

'And you've heard from Gusti? I was in Vienna to speak to Mattauch. I saw them on the ninth and they both looked well. Then I took the overnight train to Berlin. Gusti sent a telegram about it yesterday.'

'Did you not see any of it?'

'Not till I arrived in Berlin and I was going to Dahlem on the tram.'

'You have to do something, Otto.'

'What? What can I do?'

'Speak to someone. Try to get him released.'

Otto sat back in his chair. 'It's getting more and more

difficult in Berlin, Lise. It's hard keeping Strassmann in the Institute when neither of us are party members.'

'You and Strassmann are fine. It's us who aren't.' Lise picked up her cup, spilling the tea onto the white tablecloth. She dabbed at it and then left the napkin over the stain. 'Why aren't you doing anything? Why aren't any of you doing anything?'

'Why are you being like this?' Otto said, lowering his voice. 'I've come all this way to see you when Edith is in the sanatorium again, and my son has been conscripted to the Hitler Youth.'

'I know, I know, I'm sorry,' she said, dabbing at the stain again.

'I'll speak to Carl Friedrich von Weizsäcker. Maybe his father, the Baron, will be able to intervene.'

'Thank you.'

They both stared out the window, at people bent against the wind and the newsvendor across the street, holding up copies of the daily.

Lise reached across the table and grasped Otto's hand. 'Please, speak to Weizsacker.' He gave her hand a squeeze. 'I will. Now, let me cheer you up and tell you about the radium results.' He poured her some more tea and went over his and Strassmann's experiments, and how they'd even taken to sleeping in the laboratory.

'I just don't understand,' Lise said, 'how uranium's decay to radium is enhanced when it is bombarded by slow neutrons. Everything we have done has shown that slow neutrons are captured by the nucleus. You need fast neutrons to chip off an alpha particle.'

'I don't know. But that's what the results were. If only you were still with us, Lise, and it was like it used to be...'

Lise poured herself another cup of tea. 'If only,' she said.

Later, when Otto was about to board his train, Lise grasped hold of his hand. 'Repeat the experiments. Test for radium again.'

19 December 1938
Dear Lise,
We are working on the uranium substances. It is now practically 11 o'clock at night. Strassmann will be coming back at 11.45 so I can get home at long last. The thing is: there is something so ODD about the 'radium isotopes' that for a moment we don't want to tell anyone but you. The half-lives of the three radium isotopes are pretty well determined; they can be separated from all the elements except barium: all processes are correct. Except for one – unless there are some very weird accidental circumstances involved, fractionalization doesn't work. Our radium isotopes behave like barium.

Now, last week I fractioned the radium isotope thorium–x on the first floor. Then on Saturday Strassmann and I fractioned our radium isotopes with mesothorium–1 as indicator. The mesothorium–1 became enriched, our radium did not. It could still be an extremely strange coincidence. But we are coming steadily closer to the frightful conclusion: Our radium isotopes do not act like radium but like barium! I have agreed with Strassmann that for now we shall tell only *you*. Perhaps you can come up with some sort of fantastic explanation. We know ourselves that uranium can't actually burst apart into barium, which is almost half its size. But we must clear it up... So please think about whether there is any possibility – perhaps a barium isotope with much higher atomic weight than 137? If there is anything you could propose that you could publish, then it would still in a way be a work by the three of us!

We intend to write something for *Die*

Naturwissenschaften before the Institute closes because we have achieved some very nice decay curves.

    Yours, Otto

Very cordial greetings and best wishes also from me, Fritz Strassmann

On December 23, Lise travelled to Kungälvs, where she was meeting her nephew, Otto Robert Frisch. In the hotel foyer, Lise waited for him in an armchair, smoking and re-reading Otto Hahn's letter.

It was a cosy hotel, with wooden beams and a large log fire. Outside the window, the grounds were thick with snow, which reached up to the hills and down to the sea. Lise touched where the ink had blotted on the letter. She could see Otto at his desk, writing these words, dashing back to the apparatus, leaving the pen nib resting on the paper.

She wanted to be there more than anything; to observe these experiments, working all night, taking shifts, focused solely on the activities in the beaker.

Late at night, with the rest of the Institute in darkness, Otto would be standing over the beaker of radium solution, adding a small amount of barium chloride with the burette. This barium salt would solidify into crystals, locking up the tiny quantities of radium in its crystal structure.

Lise could see Otto quickly filtering the solution through one of the porcelain funnels, the minute crystals catching in the filter paper. Then he'd set the Geiger counter, listening to the click–click–click that, when measured, would plot out his beloved curves. He'd add the same amount of barium salt and wait as it crystallised again. But then he must have paused, checking the Geiger counter.

The reading was the same. Click–click–click. It should be slower, showing that with each dose of barium salt there was less radium to capture. No, the reading was about the same as it would be if the salt was capturing ordinary barium into its lattice, and not radium. He would have added more barium salt, and repeated the fractionalisation, but the result was the same. She could see Otto calling Strassmann over, and them both bending down next to the Geiger counter: click-click-click. Baffled by the results.

Lise smoothed the letter flat on her knee. She had written to Otto, saying that a reaction with slow neutrons that supposedly led to barium was very startling. The idea of such a thoroughgoing breakup of the nucleus seemed very difficult. But in nuclear physics they had experienced so many surprises that she could not unconditionally say that it was impossible.

'Aunt Lise!'

Robert walked into the foyer, holding wooden skis and wearing a fur hat.

'Robert! Look at you, you're so handsome!'

He put his skis down and hugged her, her face only reaching his chest. She always forgot he was so tall and grown up.

'Your father. Have you heard anything?' Lise said, pulling back to look at him.

'They said he can be released if he leaves the country.'

'And your mother? She hasn't replied to my last letter.'

'She's stopped leaving the house. She's scared she'll be attacked by Hitler Youths.'

'I just don't understand it all. I just don't...' She got up from her chair and looked about her. 'I need some air.'

'You'll catch your death.'

'I'm fine. I have my coat.' She buttoned it up and held out her letter. 'I've got something to show you.'

'I've been dying to tell you about my graphs.'

'First you must read this.'

He took the letter and scanned it. 'Have they made a mistake?'

'What? No. Hahn and Strassmann are too good. They don't make mistakes.'

She slipped the letter in her bag and walked outside, grasping the rail, for the stone steps were icy. At the bottom of the steps, Robert fitted his feet into the wooden skis and tied the straps. He waded forward and Lise laughed, 'Don't fall!'

'I *won't* fall, Aunty.' He pushed himself through the snow on the grass, while Lise kept to the cleared path, the cold seeping through her thin soles. They walked for a while, Lise glancing at Robert lurching on his skis, his face tense with concentration and looking for all the world like he once did as a little boy, learning to ride a bike. Finally, Lise said, 'I think it can be explained by the fact the nucleus is not just shedding a mere flake. A bit does not chip off, and barium is so much smaller.'

'Bohr,' said Robert, out of breath. 'Do you remember Bohr's idea about the nucleus being like a liquid drop, which might elongate and divide itself?'

'Yes, the uranium nucleus could be a wobbly, unstable drop, ready to divide itself at the slightest provocation,' she said, pointing to a tree trunk lying on the ground. 'Let's sit on there.' She wiped the snow off and perched on the wood.

'Like the impact of a neutron,' Robert said.

Already, Lise's hands were shaking with cold as she searched in her bag for a scrap of paper and started writing down the packing-fraction formula to work out how much energy was needed to break the surface tension of the atom.

Robert sat beside her, watching her writing, waiting, so attentive, as he used to do when she visited Gusti and Jutz in Vienna. She'd sit him on her knee and tell him about the periodic table; how the elements fitted together, and showing him where there were spaces for elements yet to be found. With pride she'd pointed out the element protactinium, just before uranium, the element that she herself had found.

And then in no time at all, he was applying for a position in Hamburg, and she had tried to be professional and objective with his reference. Too professional, perhaps. The director of the Institute wrote to her demanding to at least know whether Robert was 'a disagreeable person' or not, and she'd had to reply saying, 'No, he isn't a disagreeable person.'

'Like the impact of a neutron,' Robert said again.

'Hmm?' Lise said, looking up. 'Oh no, not like the impact of a neutron, like the slow sidling up of a neutron, Robert, like a tiny bead of condensation beside a larger one. You see the charge of a uranium nucleus is large enough to destroy the effect of surface tension almost completely. The problem is that the two drops once separated would be driven apart by their mutual electric repulsion and breaking fully would require a lot of energy, approximately 200 MeV.'

'But where would that energy come from?'

'According to the packing-fraction formula,' she said, waving her piece of paper, 'the two nuclei formed by the division of a uranium nucleus would be lighter than the original uranium nucleus by about one-fifth the mass of a proton,' Lise said. She looked out at the snow covering the fir trees, and beyond to the grey basin of the sea; she thought of her sister in Vienna, unable to leave the house and Jutz in Dachau; and Otto saying that the large numbers of Jews would surely be better treated in the camps than the political prisoners had been; of Albert congratulating her on finally leaving their 'dear and grateful fatherland', and here she and Robert were, in this icy, frozen place, so far from everyone.

'$E=mc^2$,' she said suddenly. 'According to Albert's $E=mc^2$, when mass disappears, energy is created.' Lise began to write down the equation as snow fell onto the paper. She shook it and tried to wipe the flakes away.

'Here,' Robert said, shielding the paper with his hat as she added figures to the equation. He shifted his legs to lean over her. Snow had already coated the glossy wood of the skis, and as he moved, a lump of snow slid down the rounded end to join the snow on the ground.

'200 MeV!' Lise said. 'One-fifth of a proton mass is equivalent to 200 MeV. When mass disappears energy is created. $E=mc^2$. There it is. There is the source of energy!'

Lise stared at the dampening paper as the wind picked it up, and blew it from her knee to land on the ground and disappear under the falling snow.

'Do you know what this means? This means there were no transuranes.' She pressed her hands together; she could hardly bend them now. She needed to warm herself by a fire, so she slowly stood up, every part of her aching from the cold, and walked back to the hotel, Robert following her awkwardly on his skis.

'But Aunt Lise, think about it…'

'Four years' work,' she said, turning to him. 'You don't know what this loss would mean to me.'

At New Year, Lise waved goodbye to Robert at the station as she boarded the train to Stockholm. Back in her hotel room, she switched on the paraffin heater and sat on the bed with her notes. Uranium nuclei could divide with varying proportions of neutrons and protons to form a variety of fragments including barium. There, it was clear in the equations. She was sure of her interpretation. But all that time – three, no, four years – and she had thought they had found higher elements. But there weren't any. Instead, they had found ordinary elements of middling weights. Hardly exotic. She had been so, so stupid. She had not seen what was really happening in the solution; she had not been able to interpret the results that were right in front of her. And all her life she had put her faith in the Institute and in their search for higher elements; she had ignored what was happening in

Germany so she could continue their experiments, and now people were destroying homes and businesses and killing in the street.

Lise rifled through the papers and articles on the bed until she found a piece of notepaper. She rested it on the bedside table and wrote:

1 January 1939
Dear Otto,
I begin the year with a letter to you. May it be a good year to us all. You understand, of course, that the question of the transuranes has a very personal aspect for me. If all the work of the last four years has been incorrect, it cannot be determined from just one side. I share the responsibility for it and must therefore find some way to participate in the retraction. If the transuranes disappear, you are in a much better position than I, since you have discovered it yourselves, while I have only four years of work to refute – not a very good recommendation for my new beginning.

In the morning, Lise received a letter from Robert in Copenhagen, saying that he had just talked to Niels Bohr about the discovery. Bohr was astonished he had not thought earlier of this possibility, which followed so directly from the current conception of nuclear structure. Bohr was on his way to America this week and was so excited about the results that he had installed a blackboard in his cabin.

Lise couldn't think clearly in the dank little room, so she left the hotel and walked down to the quayside. For once, the winter light wasn't murky; it was so sharp she had to shield her eyes. The river was unevenly frozen; the ice must have thawed and refrozen to form plates, but on the bank of Gamla Stan, the water still flowed and boats bobbed up and down. Further along, people were walking outside the Parliament buildings and she could hear their voices echoing across the ice. She walked along the quayside and then over the bridge to the island. Halfway across, she stopped to stare down at where the river was frozen and where it flowed. Here, as the sun melted the ice, she could see that despite the loss of the transuranes, the splitting of uranium made perfect sense; with the energy mass equation she could calculate the uranium nucleus fragmenting across the periodic table in intricate, beautiful patterns. And if she and Robert quickly published a note about their interpretation – just a page in *Nature*, then Otto could refer to it in his publication. If he wished to.

Yes, it was a drop. The atom was a drop, which could swell and swell into two, and its loss of mass would turn into energy. She dipped her gloved finger into the snow on the bridge wall and held up the flakes to her face. After the hours and days of separation and fractionalisation, Otto and Strassmann would be left with barium crystals, pure and steady in the world.

Lise shielded her eyes: over the water she could see the white orb of the sun, its fierce rays igniting the ice and quayside; merciless, searing light, blinding and burning from a fiery ball of incalculable energy that scorched and left parched whatever lay in its path.

Our Backs to the Fort

'YOU'RE MAKING IT worse.'

'I know!' I was scratching around the bites on my foot. The skin was tight and sore and my ankle was swollen from going over on cobbles. I closed my eyes so he wouldn't say anything else.

We'd had the compartment to ourselves all the way from Zagreb, James reading *Spectres of Marx* while I wrote about Ada in my notebook or stared in hazy thoughtfulness at the countryside of southern Hungary – the fields of poppy and barley, and then the industrial buildings and power stations speeding past.

I opened half an eye; James was frowning as he underlined something in his book. I got out *Austerlitz* to read again as the train shunted to a stop. Flags were hanging on the walls of the station and groups of border police with dogs were getting onto the train. We must be at the Croatian border. I could hear boots and voices in the corridor, and one of them shouting: 'Passports! Passports!'

A few minutes later, they were at our door. 'Passports, please!' The two border policemen were large and burly, with black moustaches as if they were extras in a Cold War espionage. One rubbed my photo with his finger and frowned at me. I flushed and looked away.

At Zagreb we boarded the night train to Split. We'd tried to save money by not getting a sleeper cabin, but all the second class carriages seemed to be full. We found an empty compartment and settled down. Soon after, the conductor opened the door, barking, 'Tickets!'

We gave him our inter-rail passes. He peered at them and then gestured to the air around us. 'This is first class.'

'Are these carriages all first class?' James asked. 'I think the second class ones are full.'

He motioned for us to follow him to another carriage, where he opened a compartment door and waved his torch over two sleeping men. The seats had been pulled out so they met in the middle, making a huge compartment-sized bed.

'Move, move!' the conductor ordered. They blinked, shielding their eyes, and shifted themselves towards the window.

'Sorry,' I said to them. 'Sorry.'

They grunted and turned over to sleep. James and I lay down top to toe. The compartment stank of feet and trainers, and the windows were closed but I didn't want to disturb them again.

'We so should have paid the extra,' I whispered to James.

I pulled random clothes out of my rucksack to use as blankets and a pillow and James put our rucksacks on the top rack. As the train pulled out of Zagreb, the men were soon asleep again, and James seemed to be too.

I felt restless so I pushed myself up. From the window all I could see was darkness and the occasional flash of lights.

Outside Split's station we found a cash machine, then we examined the guidebook and map. The air smelt tangy, of sea and petrol. On the left was the harbour, with boats and ferries, and ahead Split was built into the hillside. My mouth was dry and furry, and my eyes were stinging from lack of sleep. I looked at the money in my hand and then at the bread in a café window. Nearby, a man was standing on the roadside selling what looked like huge pretzels. I pointed to one with my notes.

'Careful!' James whispered. 'Don't just give him all your money.'

'I'm not giving him all my money!'

I dumped it in James' hand and marched off towards the harbour. We didn't speak while we boarded the ferry to Vis. I went to lean on the boat's railing with my back to him and watched as the island drew nearer. After a few minutes he wandered off, so I rested my chin on my arms, enjoying the wind on my face. I thought of those memories I'd kept as talismans: when we first met at a party and lay in the dawn damp of the garden, the dew soaking through our clothes while we talked and drank from a bottle of wine; attending one of his papers and him looking up to catch my eye as he spoke and blushing all the way to his neck; curled on his ragged couch, planning our itinerary with his family's hundred year old atlas, in which a lot of the world was still coloured pink.

I turned to look for him. He was also leaning on the railing and staring out to sea. As the waves washed against the side of the ferry, I thought that beneath the bickering and jibes there was some other emptiness between us.

On Vis we went into the tiny tourist office next to the harbour and rented an apartment on the seafront. When we got there, we dumped our bags and flopped on the bed. 'This place is lovely,' I said. 'I could sleep all day.'

'Sleep later,' James said. 'Let's go to the beach!'

'Wish I'd brought my swimming costume.'

We walked along the harbour, watching the retreating bulk of the ferry, its horn blowing as if saying goodbye. From somewhere a church bell tolled. It must be a Sunday. Further along, yachts and dinghies bobbed on the water, their white holds flashing in the glare of the sun. We walked past the boats and around the coast's bend to an alcove. Here, there was a small beach with pebbles and patches of sand. At the water's edge we took off our sandals and left them in a pile with our bags. The sea washed over my feet, easing the sting of my bites. James waded in, hitching up his shorts. Then he ran back, stripping off his t-shirt and shorts to just his boxers. 'Come on!' he called. 'Let's do it!'

He splashed water on me as he ran past. I wiped my face and tucked my blue dress into my knickers. That would do; I wasn't going in in just my underwear. I dipped my toes in the sea, and stopped when I saw urchins – flashes of black and red nestling between the rocks.

'Watch out for the urchins!' I called, but he was already in deep enough to swim, treading water. I went in up to my thighs, kicked my feet off the ground as quick as I could and then breaststroked further out, my dress coming loose and wafting around me.

'You still have your dress on!'

'I feel like a jelly fish.'

Lying on my back, I flipped my hands at my sides and the water lapped around my face. I felt calm for the first time in weeks, my body moving with the pull of the waves and the sun seeping through my eyelids. I drifted like this for a while, then turned onto my front and tried to doggy-paddle.

James was swimming further out, doing frontstroke the proper way with his face going from side to side in the water. He circled round and back towards me. 'And you're like a circling shark!' I called. I doggy-paddled towards him and splashed him as he went past. He turned round and kicked water all over me, then headed out again. My eyes were stinging so I swam back to shore. On the beach, I wiped my face with a tissue and wrung out my dress. Holding my arms out for the sun to dry them, I watched as James swam in.

Coming out of the water, only his arms and neck looked tanned, as if his pale skin was clothing he could take off. I still had my arms in the air. Don't, I thought, but he did; he said, 'You're going to regret swimming in that dress.'

'I'll dry off. It's boiling,' I said, then muttered, 'You're like my mother.'

'What?'

'Nothing.'

We walked around the cove, up an embankment and back onto a road. The sun was even hotter, so I put some more suncream on and passed the bottle to James. I was damp and itchy under my dress, and had to keep unsticking my knickers from my bum. James' khaki-clad self strode up the hill, leaving me behind again.

Last night in the train, I'd leaned over and whispered, 'Do you still love me?'

'Of course.'

I'd started to turn myself round so I could kiss him quietly in the darkness, but he whispered, 'You'll wake them.' I made do with stroking his leg, until he shifted and turned to face the door. Then I carried on; tiny strokes that wouldn't bother him.

He jogged back down the hill. 'See that fort up there?'

'Yeah...'

'Fancy walking up to it?'

'Erm...'

'Come on, I'll give you a piggyback.'

'OK then,' I said and climbed on. At first he went quite fast, but he soon slowed down as the road became steeper. After a while he had to put me down again. We struggled up the road, holding hands, both gasping for breath. James' back was all wet from where I'd been clinging on and my ankle really hurt, but none of that stuff mattered now; perhaps we could be good together.

Eventually, we got to where the ground flattened and there was the fort staring out to sea; a kind of watchtower. It was a square building made of grey and crumbling stones with turrets and a moat around the sides, like a mini English castle.

We stood looking up at the inscription above the

arched entrance. I couldn't make out the words, only the date: 1815.

From my bag, I fished a leaflet I'd got from the tourist office. 'It says it was built by the British in the Napoleonic wars,' I said. 'They defeated the French in 1811 in the battle of Vis. They built a number of fortresses around the island.'

'Let's go inside.'

There were three or four rooms opening out of each other. The air smelt of leaves, fungus and damp. The stone walls were covered in graffiti, and there were the remains of a fire and a dirty mattress that someone must have carried up the hill. We wandered through the dark rooms, trying to figure out what they were used for. I didn't like it so I headed to the courtyard, James following behind. Beyond was a cliff with waves crashing below, then there was a stretch of blue and the green and brown mounds of other islands. I stood as close to the cliff as I dared. 'It's beautiful here,' I said. 'If we keep our backs to the fort and look in the other direction.'

'Yeah. If we keep our backs to the fort and don't think about history.'

We followed the cliff round to a moat, climbed in and out of it, and then wandered through a copse of fruit trees to a vineyard. The vines were heavy with red grapes, and the earth between them was hard and cracked. The grapes weren't fully ripe yet, but I walked over and picked one. We hadn't eaten all day and I was suddenly starving. The grape was small and coated in white powder. I rubbed it on my dress and turned away from James so he wouldn't tell me not to eat it.

The shot made me scream. There was a smell of burning in the air. We ducked down as another shot rang out.

A man's voice came from somewhere, shouting in what must have been Croatian.

'Are we trespassing?' I whispered.

'Ssshhhh.'

Shots fired again, so we flattened ourselves on the ground, a ridge of mud almost sharp on my cheek. I held my breath and squeezed my eyes shut. Another man shouted, and the two of them seemed to be arguing. I looked up. The two men were tall, wearing white t-shirts, jeans and baseball caps, with shotguns slung over their shoulders. One was older and weathered-looking and had an Alsatian on a lead. He pointed in our direction and shouted, 'Tourist! Tourist!' and the younger man fired twice into the air. The dog barked and pulled on the lead. Then the older man pointed to a stretch of ground that was wild with grass and bushes, and had a small fence around it. He shouted some more and they turned and walked away across the field.

'Quick,' James whispered. We crawled across the ground, then ran through the trees and back towards the fort. When we got to the moat, we climbed in and hid.

We lay in the moat and listened, but there were no more shots or shouting. There was nothing at all, as if they had vanished. I was shaking and my mouth was dry, but I kept still, not wanting to make a noise rustling in my bag. After a while, James rested his head against the side of the moat. His dark hair had dried into curls and his cheeks and nose were pink with sunburn; he looked younger, boyish, with dirt on his hands and knees.

When I felt calmer, I whispered, 'Shall we go?'

'Wait, let's have a look.'

We peered over the edge of the moat. On the other side of the trees, the vineyard seemed empty, so we climbed out and walked back towards the fort. I stopped at the cliff, breathing deeply as the wind whipped my hair about my face. James stopped beside me. 'Who were they?' I asked.

'Farmers, I think.'

'Do you think they were saying it was a minefield?'

'I thought they were just arguing.'

I sank onto the grass, and James sat down a couple of feet away. I was shivering in my damp dress. I searched in my bag, but the tissues were finished, so I tried to wipe the dirt off my knees with my hands. The sun had begun to cool, and all I could hear were the waves below; even the birds seemed to have fallen silent. I wanted to reach over and hold him, but his arms were folded across his chest and his eyes were closed, his face raised towards the sun.

'What are you thinking?'

He didn't say anything.

'Go on, what are you thinking?'

He opened an eye, squinting at me. 'Do you really want to know?'

'Yes.'

'I'm thinking there's no point, really.'

'Point about what?'

'This.'

'This what?'

He shifted himself round to face me. 'OK. We've been travelling for weeks, and it's like dragging a grumpy child around. You're either silent or moody, or you drink too much and have a tantrum.'

I stared at him.

'I pity you,' he said. 'We've seen so much and you just can't enjoy it.'

'You pity me?'

'I've never been with someone who is so... unhappy.' He ran his hand though his hair and frowned at me. 'You're not going to start crying again are you?'

'No.'

'And you take everything I say as a criticism, as if I'm with you just to put you down. I can't say anything. And then you cry, and I'm just the ogre in the situation. The bad guy.'

I stood up so he couldn't see that I was beginning to cry, and headed to the courtyard.

'Yvonne!'

I stumbled into the fort, scuffing my sandals on the dirt

and kicking at the dead leaves. I wandered through the rooms that twisted in and out of each other. My eyes adjusted to the dark, so I could just make out the high walls and the grey of the stones. Then I turned a corner into complete darkness. I held my breath and reached out for a wall or anything to hold onto; the gritty stone felt soft and malleable under my fingers, and the ground was muddy and lumpy as if bodies were buried beneath. I could hear someone in here, quiet breaths, a groan and then a low voice. I thought I could see the flash of a white t-shirt. Perhaps it was one of the men with the guns. I stepped backwards till I hit another wall and then I saw a slit of light to my left. There was the mattress and the remains of the fire. I ran towards them and out through the entrance. Outside, I backed away towards the road, wiping my face with the hem of my dress.

1815

The fort would still be there, hundreds, maybe thousands of years from now, its stones moss-covered and crumbling, a reminder that people had built it to fight and conquer others. From inside, I could hear James calling my name – a hollow, fleeting sound, lost in the dank, decaying rooms.

We'll Meet Again

LEON SLIPPED OUTSIDE to smoke. It was four in the morning and only the staffroom and corridor lights were on in Lightfield's Care Home.

The air was fresh with rain and the circle of oak trees shrouded the home in darkness. When Leon had started as a care assistant ten months ago, the stink of potatoes and urine had made him gag, but somehow he'd grown used to it. As he lit his cigarette he found his hands were shaking again, so he focused on which residents needed to be checked, and who would be bathed in the morning.

Janice joined Leon on the steps. He leant over to light her cigarette. He liked Janice; even though she was small, she could lift any resident and she made them laugh – the ones that could still laugh. Plus, Janice didn't ask questions. She wasn't at all interested in Rwanda and had asked if it was in the Caribbean, though she did like to know about his wife and children. Leon often showed her photos on his phone, and told her how his son and daughter were getting on at the primary school on Langworthy Road.

'I'm not happy about it though,' Janice said, shaking her head. She'd been telling him about her daughter's boyfriend while they were putting the residents to bed. 'You know what he does? He sells exotic animals. Keeps them in his living room. He has a crocodile.'

Leon put out his cigarette. 'Crocodile?'

'I don't like Emma seeing him. I'm not being unfair, am

I? I mean you wouldn't want your daughter with someone like that?'

Leon agreed that he wouldn't.

'He has a tattoo on his neck of a diver killing a shark. I might call the RSPCA.' Janice ground out her cigarette.

'We should get back,' Leon said. They went inside to continue checking on the residents. There were forty, all with moderate to end-stage Alzheimer's and other forms of dementia. The day staff put half the residents to bed, and the night staff did the others, but since there were only four staff on duty, sometimes it was well into the small hours before they were finished. Most of the residents slept well because they were given sedatives and anti-anxiety drugs by the day nurse, but there were a couple of residents who were always up in the night and no amount of drugs could quieten them, so Leon and Janice checked on them regularly before beginning the slow process of getting them up again.

Janice was still talking about the boyfriend, and how she thought he sold the exotic animals for drugs as they passed the staffroom. Flo and Rose, the two Ugandan care assistants glanced up at Leon and giggled. Leon looked away – he always felt uncomfortable around them – and went to Mary's room. It was easy to wake the residents up, but Leon didn't want to find one lying there dead. He'd become skilled at listening to them breathe; the hollow breaths, the low snores, the twitches that showed all was well. They had to keep a special eye on the residents that had lost their ability to move their heads. Leon particularly worried about Mary suffocating in her pillow. She was only fifty-five, had a rare form of dementia, and could no longer move at all. Her husband came in every day to supervise the carers and help out, wearing shorts no matter how cold it was and shouting if they dressed her in clothes that didn't match. Sometimes her daughters came to paint her nails. Janice had told Leon that when Mary first arrived, she hit anyone who came near her, including her daughters.

He crept to her bed and leant over the rail. In the darkness, Mary's eyes stared up.

'Hello, Mary,' he said, stroking her hair. 'Can't you sleep?' Her neck looked uncomfortable, so he raised her head slightly and plumped up the cushions, then stroked her forehead. Her eyes closed so he left her to go back to the office.

'You doing your records again?' Janice popped her head out of a room. 'You and your precious records.' She laughed to herself. 'Cross off Harold. He's sleeping like a baby.' Leon nodded and turned into the office. Janice always checked on Harold because the first time Leon had attempted to help him get dressed, Harold had screamed, 'Get away from me!' and swatted Leon with his hand. Mrs Forster, the manager rushed in.

'He's hurting me!' Harold was sitting on the bed, shaking his hand at them. 'I'm not having some dirty nigger touching me.'

'It's OK, Harold,' Mrs Forster said. 'No one's hurting you.'

Mrs Forster said it was the illness speaking; sometimes it made people aggressive and not to take it personally. They'd up his drugs. But it was best someone else looked after Harold.

Leon found Mary's file and sat down at the desk with it. On the front was a photo of her, which must have been taken when she was a lot younger, or before her illness. Her short, brown hair was waved and highlighted and she was smiling at the camera. *Frontotemporal Dementia.*

He slotted her file back in the filing cabinet, and then straightened the papers on his desk. They just needed to check on Edith, Jill and Doris. Then it would be an hour before they started getting them up again.

Mrs Forster had interviewed him at this wooden desk. When she asked him about his work experience he didn't say that he used to be a mayor, that he had been responsible for the administration and organisation of a prefecture the size of Salford. Instead, when she asked why he was suitable for the job, he told her he was used to hard work, his English was excellent, as was his French and Kinyarwanda. He showed her the glowing references from his eight years of cleaning restaurants and bars in the city centre. To supplement this he had experience of caring since he and his wife had nursed his father.

Mrs Forster said that it was hard to find care assistants these days. No one wanted to do this work, and they increasingly had to rely on people like Leon. He thought she meant out of work mayors, but then he realised she was talking about immigrants.

Mrs Forster asked him to cover when the previous night shift leader resigned without giving notice. 'You have managerial and administrative potential,' Mrs Forster told him. His father had had many opinions about the importance of being a good leader, and Leon had always done his best to be one, in whatever guise this leadership took.

For example, he had started an IT course at Manchester City College and when he felt confident enough, he was going to suggest an administrative system overhaul at Lightfield's Care Home, so he could update the shift logbook directly onto the computer and this information would transfer to the residents' personal files. Then, when relatives visited, the manager wouldn't have to search through the handwritten logbook, and mistakes wouldn't be made about medication and dietary requirements.

Janice passed the doorway, carrying a pile of nappies. 'Can you check on Edith,' she said. 'I thought I heard a noise.'

'Sure,' he said, hurrying to Edith's room, where he found her pulling the sheet off the bed. Edith's short hair was sticking up and the back of her nightdress was wet. The duvet and pillows were already on the floor, and there was little else in her room – she'd already destroyed most of her belongings.

'Edith,' Leon said. 'Come on, Edith. It's OK.'

She continued yanking at the sheet.

'OK. Let's take the sheet off.' Leon helped her put the sheet on the floor. Edith pulled the duvet over it and walked out of the room. Leon found another nightdress and knickers in her cupboard and caught up with her. 'Come on, Edith. Shall we go to the bathroom? We need to change you.'

She grabbed his hand and dragged him down the corridor. They passed Janice, who called out, 'Edith's off. There she goes! Leon, that's you for the night.'

Edith beckoned, as if she had something to show him.

'Where are you going, Edith?'

They carried on down the corridor, their feet soundless on the carpet. She could go round and round for hours, sometimes taking other residents with her. Last month one had fallen and broken a hip on one of her walks.

'In here, Edith.' Leon drew her into the bathroom. 'OK, Edith. I'm going to change you.' He put on gloves, lifted her long nightdress and pulled down her knickers and pad, trying to keep her covered. She slapped at his hands. 'We need to change you, Edith. Sorry.'

He had learnt that it was important to talk to the residents and tell them what he was doing, even if he doubted they would understand. It was also important to maintain the residents' modesty. He'd had no formal training, but he'd picked up the basics by watching Janice and the other experienced carers. Janice could change and clean a resident before they had time to know what was happening.

He tried again, this time stroking Edith's arm, which she liked. He quickly lifted her nightdress and yanked down her knickers. Fortunately, it was only urine.

'You alright, Leon?' Janice peered round the door.

'Yes, thank you.'

'Here you go,' Janice said, using the tissue to wipe Edith. She sat Edith down on the toilet to change her pad and knickers. Edith started to wee, so Leon and Edith both said, 'Well done, Edith. Well done!' and she smiled up at them.

Janice gave her a final wipe and a dash of talcum powder. 'I'll take her to the communal room,' Leon said. 'It might calm her down.'

In the communal room, high-backed chairs lined the walls, a TV stood in the corner and the smell of urine was strong. Leon got the CD player off the high shelf. 'Look!' he said. 'Shall we play some music?'

She pulled at his hand to continue their walk, so he said, 'Here you are, Edith. You'll like this,' and quietly played *Wartime Memories: 100 Hits*.

Keep smiling through
Just like you always do
Till the blue skies chase those dark clouds, far away…

They sat on the chairs, and Leon stroked Edith's arm. She smiled and crossed her legs. Janice had said that when her husband visited, he brought her glasses, which she couldn't wear on her own because she'd break them, and then they danced together to this CD. 'We'll Meet Again' turned to 'The White Cliffs of Dover' as Janice came in and sat down.

'It's quite nice like this.' Janice closed her eyes. 'Don't let me drop off though.'

Leon left Janice sitting with Edith while he checked the logbook. Flo and Rose were in the staff room, sipping coffee.

'Six o'clock, girls,' he said. 'Time to get everybody up.'

'Yeah, yeah, we know,' Flo said, rolling a cigarette. 'You don't need to tell us.'

Rose raised her eyebrows at him. They stood up slowly, hands on hips, and sauntered down the corridor to the exit.

They were always like that, slightly insolent, refusing to

take any direction from him, as if he wasn't the night shift leader. As if they knew something about him.

In the office, Leon jotted down in the logbook that Edith had been agitated but 'We'll Meet Again' had calmed her down. He checked through the pages and then joined Janice to start at the other end of the corridor. Edith followed them round as they got the other residents up.

They dressed John, Joe, Margaret and Victoria. They got to Mavis and tried to sit her up, but she was still sleepy and flopped backwards. 'Come on, Mavis,' said Janice, holding the back of her head. 'It's getting up time.' Mavis muttered a jumble of words. 'I know, I know. It's far too early.' They pulled up her nightdress and Mavis tried to cover her breasts. Leon had her top waiting. 'It's OK, Mavis. Nearly there.' They attempted to get her vest over her arms, but an elbow popped out with her hand still stuck in the armhole.

They just had Mavis' vest on when calls came from the other end of the corridor. They leaned Mary back on the bed and Leon set off towards the noise.

The ambulance seemed to arrive immediately. Leon, Flo and Rose were waiting at the entrance, while Janice carried on getting the other residents up. It was nearly dawn and the road was silent apart from the chirruping of birds. The leaves on the oak trees were heavy with dew and a white cat watched from a wall. Two ambulance men climbed out with their bags. Flo started to cry when they asked what had happened. 'I went in saying, "Good morning, Harold," but he didn't respond.'

Janice came out, saying, 'I checked on him at... when was it Leon?'

'Four a.m..' Leon had the logbook and showed the ambulance man where he had written it down.

'And he was sleeping well,' Janice said. 'He seemed fine.'

The ambulance men nodded and went inside, and after

twenty minutes they brought Harold out on a stretcher, covered in a sheet.

They watched from the home's entrance as the ambulance slowly pulled out of the car park. Janice got out her cigarettes, saying, 'It happens, you know. I've seen so many die. It breaks your heart every time.'

Flo and Rose turned to Leon, as if it was his fault, Flo with her arms folded and Rose biting a nail. He ignored them and went to fill in the rest of the shift's report. They thought they knew about him, but they didn't. They knew nothing.

Leon was shaking as he sat at the desk. If anyone was going to notice if something was wrong, it was Janice. And at least he had noted it in the logbook. At least he had done that. He picked up his pen and wrote:

7.00a.m.: *Harold Tomlinson found dead. Cause unknown. Ambulance and manager called. Body taken away at 7.30a.m..*

Leon turned to Harold's file and looked at his photo. Date of Birth: 27 February 1925. Heart problem. Diagnosed with Alzheimer's in 2001. Widower. Two children: Beth and Jim Tomlinson, who visit every couple of months.

Over the months, Harold's aggression had disappeared as he spoke less and less, but Mrs Forster said that even though a person might not be able to speak, it didn't mean they couldn't feel; touch was very important and could reassure residents. Leon wasn't sure whether she meant they could still feel hatred, so he'd kept out of Harold's way.

He filed the report in the top drawer of the cabinet, placed the pens back in the desktidy, straightened the papers on the desk and sat back on the chair.

He saw then his father lying on a bed. Leon had stayed with him while his breath rasped, and the men who'd helped to write the manifesto many years before visited one by one. Days, never ending days and nights, waiting, till he felt they could remain like this forever; his father still breathing and Leon sitting by his side.

Leon rested his cheek on the desk, feeling for the woodworm and cockroach eggs that there had been in his father's desk. Leon had moved it to his office after his father died, even though the woman who cleaned the prefecture offices complained. 'Rotten' she'd say, waving her cloth at it, as if it was an abandoned carcass. 'Rotten, stinking thing.'

He remembered crouching under it as a child, while his father worked or spoke to visitors; a world of legs, sitting and standing; boots eased off; the thick stench of feet; yellowed, gnarled toenails. The long purple gown of the priest, with its muddy hem; his strange accent, and when Leon crawled out from under the desk to shake his hand, his pink skin and white, fluffy hair. The priest sweated continuously, wiping his forehead with a napkin.

'You don't understand,' the priest had said to Leon's father. 'I am with you. In Belgium, the Flemish have been oppressed. Like you, we are a majority who is a minority.'

Leon's father got out the locally brewed beer to toast to this. The priest talked of social revolution and equality; from feudalism and colonialism to democracy.

Other men came, wearing spectacles and shirts. That night in 1957, they had drafted the Bahutu manifesto, arguing till dawn about what the revolution could achieve while Leon listened from under his father's desk.

'We need equality, fairness, a proportional representation of Hutus in government.'

'Schooling for all Hutus.'

'I still don't know why *he* is here. The Catholic schools taught us to be minors and servants.'

'This good man is here to help us,' his father said.

'What the world needs to know is that the Belgian administration installed these Hamitic foreigners as rulers over us.'

'Divide and conquer.'

'Of course ethnicity should be kept on identity cards. Otherwise we won't know whether equality has been achieved. We won't know whether the Tutsi are still in control!'

They all drank the beer and talked, sometimes getting to their feet to shout at each other, while Leon went to sleep under the table, his father resting his bare feet on Leon's back. He remembered waking in his own bed at home, and in the next room, his mother was singing.

'Leon.' It was Mrs Forster at the office door. 'I'm going to the hospital to sort everything out. You should get home, you must be shattered.'

Leon stood up, as if he wasn't supposed to be at the desk.

'Yes,' he said. 'I'm going.'

The day carers were arriving. They'd want to talk about Harold, and he couldn't see Janice, so he grabbed his rucksack and went out through the kitchens. It was bright outside and already warm; the morning light felt wrong after the night shift, but he was glad to be out of there. On the road, he smelt his uniform - he stank of sweat and urine so he rummaged in his bag for his spare t-shirt, and changed into it, while a postman stared from a doorway. Leon looked away and strode round the corner to the bus stop, thinking of that Flemish priest, who had worked in his missionary school not far from the prefecture offices, until he died a few years after Leon's father.

He climbed on the bus, showed his weekly ticket to the driver, then went to find a seat on the top deck. From the back someone was playing hip hop on their phone as Leon stared out the window at the pebble-dashed houses.

He could still see his father's desk: a glass of water, various pens, a ledger and identity cards piled on top of each other, some ripped and torn, others brown with dried blood. Some cards have fallen onto the floor, so he picks them up and begins to check the names off with the names on the ledger. The names on some of the cards are obscured, so he tries to wipe them with a cloth. He sorts who is there. Who is not. Who has died. Who is not yet dead. Who needs to be found.

The identity cards keep landing on his desk, and he continues to check off their names with the names in the ledger. They pile up because there are so many of them, but some of the names aren't even in his ledger, and others will never be ticked off because the cards have been destroyed in the process.

Leon rubbed his eyes, sore with tiredness, as the bus drove past a library and bingo hall, and towards Salford Precinct.

He'd always done his job; tried to do what was best for everyone. Tonight he'd go to work early to talk to Mrs Forster about the checks they were making on the residents and how they could improve. He'd suggest updating the system and mention the programmes he'd studied at college. Before that he'd go to mass. Usually, there were only two or three people in the early evening, but he liked the emptiness of the church and how the priest's voice echoed around it. Yes, he'd go to mass on his way to Lightfield's.

The bus turned the roundabout and stopped at the Precinct. On the shop front, people were going in and out of a newsagents and a Gold Converter, and as the bus set off again and drove round the corner, he could see the market was on. It must be Tuesday morning. Working nights, he often had to remind himself what day it was.

Leon's phone beeped: *Breakfast is ready,* his wife had texted.

She always had it ready for him to eat while she took the children to school. He'd be in bed by the time she came back and she'd slip in beside him and lie there till he dozed off. She'd wake him when he moaned in his sleep – the fitful dreams he couldn't remember – and sooth him by humming old songs.

He got off the bus at the bottom of Langworthy, crossed the road and walked along the tram platform. He looked up: the sky was a clear blue with hardly a cloud; it was going to be another warm day. A tram stopped next to him and he glanced in the window, noticing a thin man, not dissimilar to him, but with a livid scar on his neck. The man turned and peered at Leon, as if he knew him. Then the man placed his hands flat on the glass and stared, squashing his face against the windowpane, trying almost to push himself through it. Leon didn't know him, or he didn't think he did, but he found that his hands were shaking. He clenched them together, then folded his arms as if to make a wall or battering ram against the man in the window, who was still staring as the tram drew away.

Notes

SOME OF THE stories in this collection were inspired by historical personages and documents. The speeches and articles in 'The Spartacist League' were drawn from Rosa Luxemburg's work, which can be found at www.marxists. org. For 'Crystal Night', I incorporated Lise Meitner's and Otto Hahn's correspondence, some of which is reproduced in Ruth Sime's *Lise Meitner: A life in Physics* (University of California, 1997). The poem '33 Bullets' is from Ahmed Arif's collection of poems, *I've Worn Out Fetters For Want of You*. This translation by Murat Nemet-Nejat is from *Eda: An Anthology of Contemporary Turkish Poetry*, edited by the translator (Talisman, 2004).

Inevitably, there are a number of ethical issues raised by such use of texts in a piece of fiction. None of the authors could be asked permission for their use, and one – Meitner's personal letters – were not intended for publication. These 'thefts' are also surrounded by other acts of voice appropriation. To write about the effects and causes of war, it is necessary to become a 'war tour' voyeur, and to adopt others' texts and histories, some of which were the histories of marginalised and disempowered groups. This kind of appropriation is a controversial issue in contemporary debates and I was increasingly aware of it as this book came together.

In her essay, 'Can the Subaltern Speak?' postcolonial theorist, Gayatri Chakravorty Spivak, warns that any attempt to speak for disempowered groups risks perpetuating the imperialism and colonialism that prevented the oppressed groups from speaking for themselves and from being heard in the first place.

While this is a risk European writers need to be wary of, I feel myself compelled to side with another postcolonial critic, Benita Parry, who argues that this 'speaking for' can be an ethical rather than appropriative act, one that does not necessarily suppress and erase difference. Parry says that occluding a representation of marginalised perspectives can in fact perpetuate that marginalisation. For Parry, fiction can bear witness to what has been silenced in history and reveal the power structures that produced this silencing. In addition, I have come to believe that in connecting these silences and rendering them vocal, fiction can reveal our own implication in such acts of silencing, either in our present position or via our cultural and national histories. This is what I have endeavoured to reveal with my stories.

But I suspect the argument will rage on. Any writing that attempts to give voice to different cultures risks more than just appropriation, but exoticisation. For Edward Said, all Western representations of 'the other' are caught up in a system of producing and regulating 'the other' for the consumption of the reader.

These dangers of exoticisation are evident in the tradition of writing that renders 'the other' as an object of scrutiny for the colonial eye, as seen in the imperialism of the eighteenth and nineteenth centuries. In researching this issue I found myself reading two nineteenth-century British colonial chroniclers, both of whom could be accused of this act: the explorer Captain John Hanning Speke, who is credited with discovering the source of the Nile, and Charlotte Manning, a little known artist and botanist whose drawings were an important step in documenting the history of the flora of Tasmania.

John Hanning Speke disseminated a fictitious tourist's

version of history – the 'Hamitic myth', which he detailed in his *Journal of the Discovery of the Source of the Nile* (1863). He used a 'myth' prevalent at the time, which claimed that the people of Abyssinia were a Caucasian tribe that had migrated from Europe, and were in fact the descendents of Noah's son Ham, while the other tribes and peoples of Africa were not even the sons of Noah, and therefore not considered human (a view that was used to legitimise slavery). Speke claimed that the Tutsi were descendents of this Caucasian tribe, who had migrated from Abyssinia, and were therefore superior to the indigenous Hutus. This was a convenient myth for the colonists because it legitimised their colonialism and reassured them that everything in Africa of 'value' actually had European and Caucasian roots. Philip Gourevitch, author of *We Wish To Inform You That Tomorrow We Will Be Killed With Our Families,* argues that this myth defined and directed racial theories and colonial policy in Rwanda and other countries. It subsequently fed back into the self-definition of the Tutsi people and became the background for the Bahutu manifesto – a key ingredient in the final story of this book and a tool in the 1994 genocide.

Such myths, then, are not merely fictions but can have real and far-reaching effects. But if the voice appropriation and exoticisation of the other is, as Spivak and Said suggest, always already underway in Western culture, the way we consume these myths can also be put under scrutiny. Indeed, it is worth mentioning the writings of Captain John Hanning Speke to see how this 'myth' came about.

In 1856, Speke made his second exploration of Africa with the famous explorer Richard Burton in search of the source of the Nile, which Speke recorded in *Blackwood's Magazine* (1859). In this account of his 'journeyings', Speke documents 'the social state and general condition' of the peoples of Africa for the interest of potential colonists: 'statesmen, clergymen, merchants and geographers.' Speke and Burton, along with numerous guides, sailors and servants, march west from Zanzibar, and in January 1858, discover Lake Tanganyika, which they travel up by canoe to the northern tip. Both explorers are suffering from various illnesses, so at Kaze, Captain Burton consents to remain behind because he is unfortunately, 'quite done up' with a fever, and cannot move without eight men carrying him in a hammock. He is furious though, about being left behind.

On 9th July 1858, Speke marches due north in search of Lake Nyanza, whose existence is rumoured and reported by the Arab merchants who travel these parts selling cloth and beads. With him is Bombay, his interpreter and valet, as well as thirty-five guides and servants, carrying their kit on donkeys (thirty-two of the donkeys die along the way).

This part of the country is lush: there are thick pastures of cotton and coffee, with 'every tropical plant that can grow,' and an abundance of 'cattle and ivory.' Speke writes that it is a virgin, ripe land that could be fruitfully cultivated if only a 'few Europeans', and in particular that civilising hand of the British, manage to reach it. Along the way they meet various villages and tribes, Speke making notes and observations in his diary on their customs, dress and physiognomy. The tone in this account is typical of the colonialist zeal to classify, define and collate, and the detail is surprising considering he is virtually blind from his illness.

By the time they near Lake Nyanza, Bombay is leading Captain Speke by the hand, and advising him where the track dips and rises. Speke's account in *Blackwood's Magazine* does not specify where they camped, but it was most likely near to the village of Sukuma where they would have traded beads for food and supplies.

At the centre of the camp, Speke lies back with a cloth over his eyes, which are swollen with the continuing infection. For the past few days he has only been able to see shadows and flashes of light, but now the lids have swollen shut. He fears the guides will lead him to a pond and claim it to be the lake, for he has been continually reminded on this trip that, as he writes: 'the natural inert laziness and ignorance of the people is their own and their country's bane.' However, Speke retains some hope for this continent since the peoples in 'Mombas up through Kikuya,' who were 'formally untameable, are gradually becoming reduced to subjection.'

The irony is, of course, that it is in this blind state that Speke is at last able to conceptualise his racial theories, which will later be published in his *Journal of the Source of the Nile*. In his mind's eye, his views spread, like a detailed, coloured map of the continent. At last, Speke knows what he will write about the Wahuma [the Tutsi]. His theory explains their more advanced feudal social structure, which would otherwise be 'inexplicable.' He can hear his own voice narrating passages to the Geographical Society. He will regale them with his descriptions and scientific analysis of the Wahuma, as the rows of wispy beards nod, taking copious notes, and Richard Burton grinds his teeth jealously in the background. 'My dear fellows,' Speke will begin:

> If the picture be a dark one, we should, when contemplating these sons of Noah, try and carry back our mind to that time when our poor elder brother Ham was cursed by his father, and condemned to be a slave of both Shem and Japeth; for as they were then, they appear to be now – strikingly, proof of the existence of the scriptures.
>
> It appears impossible to believe, judging from the physical appearance of the Wahuma, that they can be of no other race than the semi-Shem-Hamitic of Ethiopia. The traditions of the imperial government of Abyssinia go as far back as the scriptural age of King David.
>
> Most people appear to regard the Abyssinians as a different race to the Wahuma, but, I believe without foundation. Both alike are Christians of the greatest antiquity... In these countries the government is in the hands of the foreigners, who had invaded and taken

possession of them, leaving the agricultural aborigines to till the ground, whilst the junior members of the usurping clans herded cattle. There, a pastoral clan from the Asiatic side took the government of Abyssinia from its people and have ruled over them ever since, changing, by intermarriage with the Africans, the texture of their hair and colour to a certain extent, but still maintaining a high stamp of Asiatic feature, of which a marked characteristic is a bridged instead of bridgeless nose.

Speke's valet and interpreter, Bombay, aides him in drinking some more of the *pombe* – that liquor so favoured by the savages – from his canister.

Above him, Speke can hear the cry of vultures and mosquitoes buzz around his ears. Bombay leads Speke into his tent, and briefly lights a candle so he can arrange Speke's kit. Speke hears a rustling noise. 'What is that?' he says.

'Beetles, sir! Everywhere!'

Speke can feel them crawling over his legs, all heading in the same direction. 'Get rid of them!' He hits at the beetles, but they are so determined about their choice of peregrination that it seems hopeless his trying to brush them off his clothes. Eventually, he turns a cloth into a pillow and attempts to sleep.

A scrabbling in his ear wakes him. He yelps, the blindfold falling from his face, and digs in his ear with his finger. He can hear it: one of the horrid brutes is crawling and rasping in his ear. Speke tries to extract it with his finger, but only aides its immersion. The beetle seems to have become lodged and is trying to dig its way out of his tympanum. Speke feels inclined to gallop about like one of his donkeys when beset by a swarm of bees, and shake his head to get it out, but he cannot run. Not when he cannot see. So he screams and thrashes at his ear.

'Sir Sir!'

'Bombay. Give me a knife! A small knife!'

A penknife is placed in his hand. 'Help me get the damned thing out.'

Speke dips the blade into his ear and succeeds in quietening the beetle, but the knife has cut and frayed his skin, and blood bubbles from his ear.

'What? What did you say? Speak up man!'

In the morning, Speke has two bandages wrapped around his head, and an infection in his ear. The world is made of dull, hushed sounds, as if he is not marching, but swimming through murky water.

Speke has to be led continually by the hand, but by midday the party reaches the southern edge of the lake. He can feel the coolness coming off the water; he can *sense* the vastness of this mysterious inland sea.

'Let me touch it,' he says, reaching down, but he must observe the lake for himself, so he removes his blindfold and forces a puss-encrusted eye open. He has at last reached the zenith of his ambition: the Great Lake that must be the legendary and mythical source of the Nile. And although, of the great lake in question, he 'sees nothing but mist and glare,' he knows that he, only he, and not that damned Burton, has found the lake, and he will name it after his queen.

Speke's story foregrounds the danger of the colonial tourists' versions of history. As a white man of rank, his theories quickly became 'textbook' history, even for the people being colonised. Women travellers and colonists were also busy 'scribbling' their own accounts, however their writing, rather than being enshrined as history, remained unearthed - in the form of diaries and letters - until late into the twentieth century. Mrs Charlotte Manning's pamphlet *The Beauty and Rarity of The Indigenous Flora of Van Diemen's Land*, published in 1863, the same year as Speke's *Journal*, was one of the more influential of these documents and contributed to the development of late nineteenth century botany (a number of the plants drawn in her pamphlet were later brought back, housed and classified in the Royal Botanic Garden's herbarium alongside specimens collected by Darwin, Livingstone and indeed, Speke). However, Charlotte Manning's diaries, letters and notebooks have only recently been displayed at the Pankhurst Centre, Manchester, and while her story has been recovered from history, it points to other narratives that, as Spivak argues, can never be fully recovered.

While Captain John Hanning Speke was canoeing up Lake Tanganyika, Mrs Charlotte Manning recorded in her diary that she was aboard *The Eagle*, soon to land in Hobart Town, which was carrying sheep, supplies, thirty convicts and four paying passengers.

On the same day that Captain Speke discovered Lake Victoria, we find Charlotte standing on deck as the crow's nest shouts, 'Land!' From drawings of her fellow passengers we can imagine how she might have looked: wrapped in a lacy blue shawl, holding a parasol, now battered from four months at sea, its blue and white frills tinged grey and stiff with salt. I can picture her re-pinning her dark hair as the wind slaps it about her face, the heat and the wind searing her cheeks. In her diary she regrets staying out too long in the sun; her complexion is growing ruddy, but she confesses it is too thrilling to watch the ship's mates going about their work, scurrying up and down the masts, and scrubbing the decks. The speck on the horizon is growing and she can make out mountains, the jagged shore and the docks of Hobart Town. She twirls her parasol in excitement. A brand new land.

In a letter to her mother, dated 8th December 1858, Manning writes:

> Mother, I'm afraid you would find the sea voyage irksome. The ship is as dirty as we presumed it would be due to it being an old coal boat. An air of coal dust

seems to trail in the ship's wake. The cabin is cramped and not the most clean, and swarms with woodlice. Despite these deprivations, I find seafaring – and I do feel like a seafarer – to be the most exciting of distractions. If I do not move from my position, the captain lets me remain on the rim of the quarterdeck. He is most courteous, though the other mates are coarse in their manners and as slovenly and idle as one could imagine.

I am managing to draw a little, despite the rocking of the ship. In fact, one could say that I have found both my sea legs and my sea fingers! I have enclosed a few sketches of the ocean, seabirds, and parts of the ship.

For the first few days the other passengers have been completely indisposed due to seasickness, but they have since recovered their equanimity. Mr and Mrs Clouth are kind, though Doctor Brignose, who is a professor from Oxford University, is trying to educate me about the colony. His discourses at dinner on bone collecting are interminable. Yesterday, there was a weevil on his plate, and I didn't dare interrupt him telling me about savages' skulls while he ate it.

I have sad news to tell you mother. My maid, Josie, succumbed to fever and passed away a few weeks into the voyage. I know you will be concerned about my well-being, but the Clouths have taken me under their wing and Mrs Clouth has nominated me as her chief companion.

There are details she doesn't mention in the letter, but can be found in her diary: Josie dying in Charlotte's cabin, the rancid smell of the hold, and seeing bodies thrown into the sea with only a few lines from a prayer book. She writes, 'When I wake in the night, I see Josie sinking to the bottom of the ocean, the sheet unravelling like a spool, her hair cascading, her eyes open and staring.'

Charlotte says little about her husband, Charles Manning, in either the voyage diary or her letters. In the library of Hobart Town, the parish documents record his career and work for the New Land Company. He married Charlotte in 1855 and immediately took his post. She joined him a year later. After Charlotte's death, he would remain a widower for a number of years and finally marry a freed convict woman called Grace Jones. Charlotte's earlier diaries note that they met amidst the citrus trees in the orangery of Heaton Park Hall. Lady Mary Stanley, a friend of Charlotte's mother, had long encouraged Charlotte's interest in botany, and introduced her to Charles with the words: 'You are both voyagers.'

Charlotte describes him as 'tall' and 'swarthy' and 'the epitome of a hero in a romance'. There are conflicting accounts of how he proposed a few weeks later. In one letter she describes it as 'extremely romantic as we were hidden behind the lemon trees,' and all on 'one knee' (to Louisa Jane, 1856), but her diary glosses over their meeting with, 'we are getting married. At least I will be able to leave Manchester.'

In her diary entry dated 5th June 1856, she writes:

> Charles is so excited about his new employment. I am glad to go with him. I detest Manchester. There must be somewhere different. I can hardly breathe here, as if there are a thousand eyes watching, hidden in every corner. I am so glad we are escaping this country together. I hope to study the flora in Van Diemen's Land. Yesterday, while we were sojourning on the bench in the orangery, Charles said Van Diemen's was 'unclaimed land,' and fairly crushed my hands in his. 'Darling, it's a tabula rasa, there for the picking. It's all ours. When you arrive, there will be our home in

the most beautiful land, with all the flowers you can draw.'

Charlotte is at her position on the quarterdeck, waiting for her sea chests to be brought up. The ship bustles with men carrying bags and boxes, but she is apprehensive as they approach the port. Her diary describes the docking:

> Hobart Town is situated on the rising banks of the Derwent, with green meadows, gardens and pleasant country residences, and beyond there are the snowy mountain peaks of Mount Wellington.
>
> On the harbour, there was no sign of Charles, though his convict-servant, Johnson, was there to meet me. He is a large man, with a bulbous, pock-marked face. We travelled to the residence on horseback, along terrible roads, which were merely indents in the dirt. Our house is not situated in the lovely Hobart Town at all; it is a number of miles away, in a lonely valley, surrounded by 'bush'. At first I was alarmed at this, but then I thought how wonderful it will be to live in a secluded location. The house is made of rickety wooden flaps, as if it could be lifted clean off the ground.

As Johnson shows her around, he says Charles will not return until the evening. She is dismayed at this news, and tries not to look aghast at the small kitchen and barely furnished parlour, or the three cramped bedrooms; one floor is not a house. Her room is pretty enough, with a large bed, washstand and chest of drawers.

It is early evening when Charles returns with three other men on horseback, carrying rifles. She waves from the doorway, but he does not seem to see her. He shouts to the men as they go past to the stables. She writes:

He did not say where he had been. He went to wash before he would greet me properly. Then he strode into the parlour and grasped my hands, brushing his lips on my cheek. I stood on tiptoe, but he turned away and poured himself a drink of whisky.

After dinner, he took my hands and said, 'My dearest Charlotte. We live in difficult times. We are under attack from the savages.' He told me that the savages were cruel, dangerous and unpredictable, and ambushing the settlers. There would always be someone at the house to protect me, but he would show me where the pistol was kept. 'We are at war,' he said.

I feel very much afraid.

That night, as she is getting ready for bed, Charles goes out again and Charlotte can hear men shouting. She tiptoes downstairs, her shawl around her, and makes her way to the kitchen door, but Johnson says, 'Go back to bed, Madam. It is nothing.'

There is no mention of her fear of attack in her letters to her mother. Instead, she writes of the Reverend Thomas Atkins and Mr Backhouse coming to dinner. She states, 'They had such an altercation about the savage tribes and how they will disappear before the civilised races. One says it is divine will and the other that they are the link between man and the monkey tribe! However, you don't want to hear of that dreary business, Mother. You will be pleased to know that the climate is much like home, though the seasons are all back to front.'

Her diary reveals a little more. 'I don't really feel married,' she writes. 'Charles is hardly at home. I am lonely, but I prefer his absence. The only company I have is Johnson, with his horrid porridge face. He is maid, cook and butler. He speaks to me as if he is the one giving the commands.'

During this time Charlotte sets about drawing and

documenting the local flora, though she is told not to venture far. Her diary states:

> I have to content myself with whatever I find in the vicinity. I am cooped up. A hen in a hen house, though I am glad we have few visitors because they invariably bring news of Hobart Town. In a letter from Mrs Clouth, I was distressed to hear slander about a woman who had lived here for years without ill repute. Apparently, she had had some affair in England. Someone had travelled all the way here to inform people of this! I can barely induce myself to reply to her fifteen-page letter.
>
> Around the house the valley is rich and verdant; a stream wanders nearby, interrupted by huge rocks; shrubs and trees hang over and dip into its shady pools, and all around there is flora and foliage, which I have already begun collating and drawing. Towards the hills there are clusters of gum trees, with their white gnarled and twisted roots, which pertain an uncanny aspect, as if they could come alive.
>
> My favourite is the Waratah bush, a lovely shrub or bushy tree, which has dark-green foliage and bright red flowers of loosely clustered trumpet florets.

I imagine Charlotte wearing a wide-brimmed hat. She is collecting flowers, picking off stems and buds to be pressed, drawing them in pencil, and using a watercolour wash. She sits with her sketchpad for hours during the day. She feels a calmness, a serenity here, something she never felt back home. Her diary does not reveal why she wanted to leave England, but she writes, 'Perhaps I am a type of convict too, paying a penance, but it is a penance paid in paradise.'

Charlotte did not live long in this paradisiacal jail. After her death, *The Rarity and Beauty of the Indigenous Flora of Van Diemen's Land* was published in Britain, at her mother's behest. All that is known about her passing is contained in a letter from Charles Manning to Charlotte's mother:

> Dear Mrs Brown,
>
> It causes me great pain to be the one to inform you of Charlotte's demise. We were exceedingly happy in our marriage, but two months ago, Charlotte was gravely ill. Her exact illness is unknown, but the physician thought it was a type of fever. She has been buried in the graveyard on the property. I enclose her pamphlet and drawings. You might be able to do something with them. My deepest condolences and sincerest wishes,
>
> Charles Manning.

Before her death, Charlotte went through her own lapsarian fall, becoming both silenced and complicit in the long history of silencing. In one of her notebooks there is an unfinished drawing of an outhouse. In the background, there are hills swathed in clouds, and in the foreground there are stables, a stream and to the right a small wooden building. The door is closed and there are no windows. Half the building is carefully shaded in, using cross-hatching and smudging, but the rest is just an outline.

Perhaps it is while drawing the outhouse that Charlotte wonders what is inside. I can see her there with her stool and easel. No, maybe she does not use an easel since the notebook is small. She is drawing on her knee and there is a stand for her parasol to keep the sun off her cheeks. It is quiet, for as usual there is only Johnson at home. Charlotte is sweaty and prickly under her long-sleeved blouse and full skirt. She is squinting in the sun and shading in part of the building. This is when she hears a noise. She can barely make it out. She glances around and hears it again. A moaning: a strange, low cry coming from the outhouse. She writes in her diary before tearing the page out: 'There was a noise and I was curious about it. I wish, God preserve me, that I had not ventured to find it out.'

She leaves her parasol and notebook, and picks her way through the grass to the building. Yellowed bushes have spurted up around the door. Perhaps she bends to smell a flower. She pulls at the lock. The door is bolted from the outside. She must have got a key from the house. Perhaps she takes the bunch of keys from the kitchen and tries each key till one fits the lock.

As the door opens, the smell hits her, something bad, like rotting meat. She coughs and covers her mouth. The doorway shines a square of light into the room, revealing hay spread over the ground. She pushes the door open and sees it: a figure lying on the floor, its legs chained together. There is a moan and Charlotte steps forward. It is a woman, though she hardly seems a woman; her hair is cut short and she is thin, the skin taut on her cheekbones. She is lying on her side and a scrap of cloth is drawn over her with dark stains. The woman lifts her head and raises her hands to her face. She tries to say something, but her voice is a scratch, a mutter. Charlotte cannot make it out.

'I stepped back,' she might have written in her diary. 'I cannot describe how I felt at that moment, but then I heard a voice behind me. 'What are you doing here?' It was Johnson.

At the touch of his hand on her elbow, her knees buckle. 'Come away. You should not be here,' he says. He grips her arm and she falls against him. He pulls her out of the building and into the sunlight and then he turns and locks the door.

She can feel herself crying as they walk back to the house. By the door she stops. 'I told him to give me the keys,' she insists on that page of her diary. 'The woman needed water. But he shook his head and said, "I'm afraid I can't. It's Master Charles' orders." So I let him lead me into the house.'

She stumbles to her bedroom. She takes off her hat, undoes her blouse buttons and splashes water on her face. She lies on her bed, quite still, until her husband returns in the early evening. Charlotte listens for his tread in the corridor and sits up straight when he knocks at the door.

'Yes,' she says.

Charles throws her bedroom door open. 'Do not dare,' he says from the doorway, 'to interfere in my business. Do not meddle around any building that is not the house.' Then he sits next to her on the bed and sighs, 'You have much to learn, darling. There are many things happening that you do not understand. I think from now on Johnson should remain with you when you are outside of the house.'

Charlotte nods, but pulls her hands away from his.

'Come,' he says. 'If things calm down, I'll organise an expedition for your flowers.'

Charlotte's only surviving mention of the incident in her diary appears in an otherwise unexplained passage:

> I dreamt again of the outhouse. I am at the door but I do not have a key. I drop my notebook and pull and scratch at the lock. I hit my hands against the wood till splinters cut my palms, because inside there is a terrible screaming, and the door will not open.

ALSO AVAILABLE FROM COMMA:

The Madman of Freedom Square

Hassan Blasim

978-1905583256
£7.99

'Perhaps the best writer of Arabic fiction alive...'
— The Guardian

From hostage-video makers in Baghdad, to human trafficking in the forests of Serbia, institutionalised paranoia in the Saddam years, to the nightmares of an exile trying to embrace a new life in Amsterdam... Blasim's stories present an uncompromising view of the West's relationship with Iraq, spanning over twenty years and taking in everything from the Iran-Iraq War through to the Occupation, as well as offering a haunting critique of the post-war refugee experience.

Together these stories represent the first major literary work about the war from an Iraqi perspective.

Long-Listed for the 2010 Independent Foreign Fiction Prize

'Blasim moves adeptly between surreal, internalised states of mind and ironic commentary on Islamic extremism and the American invasion... excellent.' — The Metro

'Blasim pitches everyday horror into something almost gothic... his taste for the surreal can be Gogol-like.'
— The Independent

www.commapress.co.uk

The Book of Istanbul

A CITY IN SHORT FICTION
Ed. Jim Hinks & Gul Turner

978-1905583317

£7.99

Featuring:
Türker Armaner - Murat Gülsoy - Nedim Gürsel - Muge Iplikci - Karin Karakasli - Sema Kaygusuz - Gönül Kivilcim - Mario Levi - Özen Yula - Mehmet Zaman Saçlioglu

Istanbul. Seat of empire. Melting pot where East meets West. Fingertip touching-point between two continents.

Even today there are many different versions of the city, different communities, distinct peoples, each with their own turbulent past and challenging interpretation of the present; each providing a distinct topography on which the fictions of the city can play out.

This book brings together ten short stories from some of Turkey's leading writers, taking us on a literary tour of the city, from its famous landmarks to its darkened back streets, exploring the culture, history, and most importantly the people that make it the great city it is today. From the exiled writer recalling his appetite for a lost lover, to the mad, homeless man directing traffic in a freelance capacity... the contrasting perspectives of these stories surprise and delight in equal measure, and together present a new kind of guide to the city.

www.commapress.co.uk

ALSO AVAILABLE FROM COMMA:

The Shieling

David Constantine

978-1905583218
£7.99

'Perhaps the finest of contemporary writers in this form.'
— The Reader

Tree-climbing students, volunteering soldiers, island-bound recluses... The characters in David Constantine's remarkable new collection are united by an urge to absent themselves, to abscond from the intolerable pressures of normal life and withdraw into strange ideas, political causes, even private languages. Viewed from without, they appear sometimes absurd — like the vicar who starts conversing with the Devil when his wife leaves him — sometimes tragic — like the vision of a suicide being fished out of the River Irwell. Such is the force of Constantine's compassion, however, we cannot help but follow each character deep into their isolation.

*WINNER of the BBC National Short Story Prize 2010 *

*SHORTLISTED for the 2010 Frank O'Connor International Short Story Award *

'So good I'll be surprised if there's a better collection this year...' — The Independent

www.commapress.co.uk